SOME LOOK
BETTER DEAD

THE CLASSIC HANK JANSON

The first original Hank Janson book appeared in 1946, and the last in 1971. However, the classic era on which we are focusing in the Telos reissue series lasted from 1946 to 1953.

The following is a checklist of those books, which were subdivided into five main series and a number of "specials".

The titles so far reissued by Telos are indicated by way of an asterisk.

Pre-series books

When Dames Get Tough (1946)
Scarred Faces (1946)

Series One

1 This Woman Is Death (1948)
2 Lady, Mind That Corpse (1948)
3 Gun Moll For Hire (1948)
4 No Regrets For Clara (1949)
5 Smart Girls Don't Talk (1949)
6 Lilies For My Lovely (1949)
7 Blonde On The Spot (1949)
8 Honey, Take My Gun (1949)
9 Sweetheart, Here's Your Grave (1949)
10 Gunsmoke In Her Eyes (1949)
11 Angel, Shoot To Kill (1949)
12 Slay-Ride For Cutie (1949)

Series Two

13 Sister, Don't Hate Me (1949)
14 Some Look Better Dead (1950) *
15 Sweetie, Hold Me Tight (1950)
16 Torment For Trixie (1950)
17 Don't Dare Me, Sugar (1950)
18 The Lady Has A Scar (1950)
19 The Jane With The Green Eyes (1950)
20 Lola Brought Her Wreath (1950)
21 Lady, Toll The Bell (1950)
22 The Bride Wore Weeds (1950)
23 Don't Mourn Me Toots (1951)
24 This Dame Dies Soon (1951)

Series Three

25 Baby, Don't Dare Squeal (1951)
26 Death Wore A Petticoat (1951)
27 Hotsy, You'll Be Chilled (1951)
28 It's Always Eve That Weeps (1951)
29 Frails Can Be So Tough (1951)
30 Milady Took The Rap (1951)
31 Women Hate Till Death (1951) *
32 Broads Don't Scare Easy (1951)
33 Skirts Bring Me Sorrow (1951) *
34 Sadie Don't Cry Now (1952)
35 The Filly Wore A Rod (1952)
36 Kill Her If You Can (1952)

Series Four

37 Murder (1952)
38 Conflict (1952)
39 Tension (1952)
40 Whiplash (1952)
41 Accused (1952)
42 Killer (1952)
43 Suspense (1952)
44 Pursuit (1953)
45 Vengeance (1953)
46 Torment (1953) *
47 Amok (1953)
48 Corruption (1953)

Series Five

49 Silken Menace (1953)
50 Nyloned Avenger (1953)

Specials

A Auctioned (1952)
B Persian Pride (1952)
C Desert Fury (1953)
D Unseen Assassin (1953)
E One Man In His Time (1953)
F Deadly Mission (1953)

SOME LOOK BETTER DEAD

by

HANK JANSON

This edition first published in England in 2003
by Telos Publishing Ltd
61 Elgar Avenue, Tolworth, Surrey, KT5 9JP, England
www.telos.co.uk

Telos Publishing Ltd values feedback.
Please e-mail us with any comments you may have
about this book to: feedback@telos.co.uk

ISBN: 1-903889-82-0

This edition © 2003 Telos Publishing Ltd
Introduction © 2003 Steve Holland.

Novel by Stephen D Frances
Cover by Reginald Heade
Silhouette device by Philip Mendoza
Cover design by David J Howe
This edition prepared for publication by Stephen James Walker

With thanks to Steve Holland.
www.hankjanson.co.uk

Internal design, typesetting and layout by David Brunt

The Hank Janson name, logo and silhouette device
are trademarks of Telos Publishing Ltd

First published in England by S D Frances, January 1950

Printed by Antony Rowe Ltd,
Bumpers Farm Industrial Estate, Chippenham, Wilts, SN14 6LH

1 2 3 4 5 6 7 8 9 10 11 12 13 14 15

British Library Cataloguing in Publication Data. A catalogue
record for this book is available from the British Library.

PUBLISHER'S NOTE

The appeal of the Hank Janson books to a modern readership lies not only in the quality of the storytelling, which is as powerfully compelling today as it was when they were first published, but also in the fascinating insight they afford into the attitudes, customs, modes of expression and, significantly, morals of the 1940s and 1950s.

We have therefore endeavoured to make *Some Look Better Dead,* and all our other Hank Janson reissues, as faithful to the original edition as possible. Unlike some other publishers who, when reissuing vintage fiction, have been known to make editorial changes to remove aspects that might offend present-day sensibilities, we have left the original narrative absolutely intact. So if, in the original edition, Hank made, say, a casually sexist remark about women – as he does on occasion – then that is what you will read in the Telos edition as well.

That's just the kinda guy Hank was.

Which brings us to a point about language. The original editions of these classic Hank Janson titles made quite frequent use of phonetic "Americanisms" such as "kinda", "gotta", "wanna" and so on. Again, we have left these unchanged in the Telos reissues, to give readers as genuine as possible a taste of what it was like to read these books when they first came out, even though such devices have since become sorta out of fashion.

The only way in which we have amended the original text has been to correct obvious lapses in spelling, grammar and punctuation – we have, for instance, added question marks in the not-infrequent cases where they were omitted from the ends of questions in the original – and to remedy clear typesetting errors. So in the Telos edition of *Some Look Better Dead,* the character Johnny Peters retains that name throughout, whereas in the original edition he became Johnny Wilson in one sequence.

Lastly, we should mention that we have made every effort to trace and acquire relevant copyrights in the various elements that make up this book. If anyone has any further information that they could provide in this regard, however, we would be very grateful to receive it.

INTRODUCTION

You could be forgiven for thinking that this was a nasty little book written by a dirty-minded author. You wouldn't be the first to think so. *Some Look Better Dead* was one of the top twenty most burned books fifty years ago, with forty-nine destruction orders issued against it in the period 1950-1953. Most of those orders would have been for one or two copies at a time; a handful at most. A drop in the ocean compared with even the initial print-run, which would have been around 50,000 copies. A reprint was rolling off the presses about six months after the title's first appearance in January 1950; further reprints followed in 1951 and 1952; and a later reissue under the title *Play It Quiet* (Roberts & Vinter E185, 1962) probably pushed the circulation up to around 100,000 to120,000 in the UK alone.

These figures may not sound astonishing in these days of *Harry Potter*, but in 1950 they were. Added to that, a new Janson novel was appearing approximately every six weeks and achieving a similar sales performance; reissues of older titles were also selling out; and cumulative sales reached a million books a year during 1950-1951, and rose even higher in 1952-1953.

Whatever Janson was doing, a lot of people obviously felt he was doing it right.

Trying to discern what attracted readers from a distance of more than fifty years is no easy task. On the surface, the books have a simple formula of violence and explicitly implied sexuality, perfectly encapsulated in the wonderful artwork covers by Reginald (Heade) Webb. But anyone who cares to look a little deeper into the books and compare them with any of Janson's rivals from that era will soon discover that they had a complexity that was not to be found in any of his paperback contemporaries. The author, Stephen Frances, in writing as and about Hank Janson, was able to create a character whose viewpoint readers could follow throughout the series and with whom they could become involved, letting themselves view Hank's world through the keyhole of Frances's writing.

Some Look Better Dead [*] lulls its readers before turning on them. As the story opens, we get a brief look at the hustle and bustle of daily life in a busy newspaper office, and a brief reintroduction to some of the characters who would thread through the Janson saga – this being the second tale of Hank in the role of a *Chicago Chronicle* crime reporter. The length of the books (around 35,000-40,000 words) never allowed for anything more than a cursory exploration of the newsroom offices or their inhabitants, unless they were to play a central role in a particular story. That's a shame, because the offices of the *Chicago Chronicle* were filled with many potentially interesting characters: Jim Conway, the cigar-smoking sports writer; Charlie Lester, the paper's political correspondent; Jenny, the bespectacled office typist with a crush on Hank; even the sour, blue-uniformed elevator boy who manages to get the better of Hank in their daily bad-mouthing badinage. The Janson books needed to get right on with the action, often at the expense of background development.

Some Look Better Dead has a relatively slim plot, and this allowed Frances the opportunity to open the story with some of his most humorous writing. Hank, despite being one of the smartest reporters on a newspaper known to the majority of America's 157 million inhabitants, is as human as his readers, and sometimes isn't the sharpest tool in the box. Given to flashes of green-eyed jealousy and fits of anger, he often aggravates an already tense situation by saying something inappropriate where he ought to choose his words with more care and subtlety. Whether that is down to deliberate provocation – testing the people he is talking to – or simple insensitivity is left to the reader to decide. The fact is, Hank is prone to all human frailties, including plain stupidity. Even as he is smartly figuring out the complexities of the mystery surrounding the disappearance of Treasury Department employee Ellis Tundall, he suffers one of those dimming-of-the-bulb moments that puts his life in danger.

Stephen Frances played with Hank's all-too-human nature, sometimes to hilarious effect. How many heroes of a long-running

---

[*] Or *Some Look Better – Dead* as the original cover gave, following the inflexion of the doctor who gets to speak the line towards the end of the book.

series of novels would lose an argument with an elevator boy, or be allowed to make a fool of themselves at a fashion show? How many would skim their hat towards a hat-peg only to have it land in the waste-paper basket?

Within his fictional world, Hank's character is so well defined to the other characters around him that he can be easily manoeuvred – in the opening chapter, see how quickly the Chief can locate and pull the right strings to get Hank back on board, after he angrily quits for being pulled off a story. As usual in a Janson novel, the female characters seem to know by some gestalt empathy precisely how to manipulate Hank the moment they meet him. This could only have been a deliberate choice by author Frances, and it is particularly noticeable in this novel since the central theme of the whole book is humiliation – and Hank, above all others, is constantly humiliated. Within the first page or two of the book, Hank has been the victim of the elevator boy's back-chat ("I had the uneasy feeling I got the worst of it every time") and been verbally abused by his colleague Sheila Lang ("You big ape!"). Eventually he finds himself bound and gagged and forced to listen to the violent lovemaking of his captors.

The light-hearted introduction to the main story, taking up the first quarter of the book, gives way to a shocking and uncomfortable storyline centred around the brutal relationship of Edward and Fay Trice. There are no explanations offered, and the story ends on a chilling note, made more so because the author presents no glib solutions to guide the reader's feelings.

It is easy to explain away the attraction of Eddie and Fay as that of a sadomasochistic relationship. Eddie is clearly a sadist who enjoys humiliating people, primarily his wife. Fay, however, does not enjoy the violence in the relationship. Unlike in classic masochistic fiction – of which Leopold Sacher-Masoch's *Venus in Furs* immediately springs to mind, since it was Sacher-Masoch who inspired the term "masochism" – Fay does not dream of being bound or hurt or humiliated as a method of achieving sexual excitement. She does not encourage her partner to indulge in the extreme violence he enjoys. The successful sadomasochistic relationship is controlled by the masochistic partner, who sets boundaries to which the sadistic partner adheres, almost like a contract between the two that sets out limits to the suspense, anxiety and prolonging of any suffering. In this case, Fay has signed no contract: Fay is nothing more than a slave in the hierarchy of her relationship with Eddie. If Fay uses the violence to realise her secret desires (or to punish herself for having secret desires), this is not made clear.

To explain away Fay's obsessive love for Eddie as a sexual perversion would be to miss the point – indeed, when the abuse becomes too extreme, Fay tries to kill herself; and, when that fails, she obtains a divorce from her husband. Fay shows many of the tendencies seen in real-life cases of abuse: although we do not know much about her background other than that she is the sister of a highly successful model and that her parents are dead, we do see that there is resentment between Fay and her sister, an intense need for love and affection (she almost throws herself on Hank the moment they meet), an inability to set and enforce interpersonal boundaries, a low self esteem and other signs that Fay has a co-dependent personality disorder. She is addicted to her former husband who, in common with other abusers, has isolated his partner from all social contact by sacking his servants and locking her up. His compulsive and reckless behaviour, uncontrollable temper and antisocial temperament are typical of an abusive nature.

Fifty years ago, spousal abuse was almost unheard of. Even now, unbelievable as it may seem, fewer than twenty countries in the world treat non-consensual sex within marriage as a crime; forced sex within marriage was only recognised as rape in the UK in 1991, and marital rape was finally included in the criminal statutes of all fifty states in the USA in 1993. While sexual perversion had been the subject of study since Richard von Krafft-Ebing published *Psychopathia Sexualis* in 1886, it was not a widely discussed topic in the 1950s, being usually confined to clinical studies and textbooks about sexual psychology.

Frances, however, was well aware of his subject matter. As an aside from his writing and publishing of Hank Janson, he also distributed books from his office in Southampton Row – the kind of books that were highly priced and posted out in plain brown wrapping. Amongst these could be found books on sexual behaviour (including the Kinsey Report), auto-eroticism and

The 1962 reissue of *Some Look Better Dead* by Roberts & Vinter Ltd - Hank's then publishers - came under the new title *Play It Quiet*.

sexual compulsion, as well as one published by Frances in a limited edition of 2,000 signed and numbered copies entitled *Sex and Sadism* by the pseudonymous Val Vane.

There can be no doubt that Frances was making a conscious study of sexual abuse in *Some Look Better Dead*; the characters are too well defined for him to have simply stumbled upon the theme. The novel is too uncomfortable and downbeat to be considered as simply pandering to the lower instincts of his readers; although there are parts of it that do precisely that. The cover was certainly pandering to certain tastes – three of the first four covers in the Second Series of Janson novels were bondage covers – and Frances could be accused of fetishising the violence in the novel when he wrote lines like: "His fist flashed, there was the meaty sound of knuckles smacking against flesh, and Fay sprawled over backwards on the floor." But given the context of the novel, such lines are too shocking to be stimulating.

Frances also deliberately turns the tables on his hero. At the fashion show in the opening section of the book, Hank is surrounded by models wearing very little and takes the opportunity to describe them in loving detail: "The model had reached the beginning to the parade aisle. She turned slowly, took two paces, which brought her just in front of me, and turned again slowly. The panties were tailored, and fitted over her hips with a tantalizing emphasis."

Later, Frances turns this situation on its head when Hank himself becomes the object of desire: "Fay sat up and looked at me cheekily. Her eyes wandered over my body approvingly, and I got some idea of just how a dame can feel when she is being eyed up by a guy who wants to make her."

Sexual attraction and desire were part and parcel of the paperback crime thriller of the early 1950s, but while most authors never strayed beyond the power fantasies of tough guys and their nymphomaniac molls, the world of Hank Janson was never quite as secure. Hank goads, aggravates and annoys many of the people he meets – not the suave actions of your average hero. He is objectified and finds that it makes him feel uncomfortable. And in the end, he does not get the girl.

All this from a novel too easily dismissed as a nasty little book written by a dirty-minded author. Frances often confronted his readers with unpleasant, even distressing, storylines, and as often made no attempt to confabulate some lame explanation for the actions of his characters. Perhaps it was this danger – that you might find yourself caught up in something more than a simple thrill-ride of murder and mayhem – that brought the readers back time and time again in such great numbers.

Steve Holland
Colchester, July 2003

CHAPTER ONE

The sidewalk was jammed with the usual mid-morning hustle and bustle of clerks, businessmen, commercial travellers and typists on their way to or returning from coffee. It was a grand morning, and I paused beneath the *Chronicle* clock, took two or three deep breaths and felt that the world was good. The revolving doors of the *Chronicle* were continuously turning, admitting and ejecting the never-ending flow of folks who wanted to visit the newsroom, insert a classified advertisement, make an enquiry about a competition, or even to try to sell the Editor a news story.

As I climbed up the steps towards the swing doors, Jim Conway, the sports writer, came out at a hell of a lick and almost knocked me over.

"Hiya, Hank," he yelled. "In a hurry."

"Hiya," I said.

"Chief's been looking all over for you," he yelled over his shoulder.

He can wait, I thought to myself as I picked my way through the crowded ground-floor office and thumbed for the elevator.

The elevator boy wore a bright blue uniform with gold buttons. "Has little boy blue found his horn yet?" I asked.

He scowled as he closed the gates behind me. "You're late, hawkeye," he commented.

It was my turn to scowl. "Lay off that hawkeye business," I warned him, "or I'll beat your head in."

"You being such a smart guy," he sneered, "I thought maybe you'd be looking for little boy blue's trumpet yourself, just so you can blow it, good and loud."

"You're a smart guy, yourself," I told him. "Maybe if you could read and write, you'd get to be President someday."

"Reading's no good to anyone," he said sourly. "Especially reading the stuff that's printed nowadays."

"Maybe we ought to ask you what to print," I suggested sarcastically.

"You could do a whole lot worse than that."

The lift slowed to a stop, he pulled a lever and the doors slid open softly. I stepped out and he said softly: "Better put a move on. I heard the Chief was looking for you."

The lift gates slid shut and I stood staring at them for several seconds. Every time I came up in the lift, I got a line of cross-talk from that operator. I had the uneasy feeling I got the worst of it every time. I shrugged, walked along the corridor and opened the door into the newsroom.

Jenny, the newsroom typist, was on her feet waving at me as soon as I entered. "Mr Janson," she cooed. "Oh! Mr Janson, can I see you a moment? It's very urgent."

I skimmed my hat across my desk, aiming for the hat-peg. I missed by six inches and the hat fell into the waste-paper basket. I tried that trick every morning. Once in a while I pulled it off.

I went over to Jenny. "Something special?" I asked.

She fluffed her hair with one hand, smoothed her skirt with the other and gazed at me tenderly through her thick-lensed spectacles before she coyly dropped her eyes.

"Hank," she said softly, as though it was a great secret just between her and me, "the Chief wants to see you. It's urgent."

"Jungle drums brought me the message an hour ago," I told her.

"Oh! I didn't know." She flicked her eyes up towards me again, and she'd lost her shy look now and looked just artful. "I thought you ought to know, Hank," she said, and her forefinger began to trace patterns on the desk-top. She acted like a seventeen-year-old just out of college.

"That's okay, Jenny," I said brusquely. "Thanks for the tip-off." I got away from her as quickly and as graciously as I knew how. Jenny was a good worker. But she was a good talker too, and for some reason, of all the guys in the newsroom, she had to sort me out as the guy she wanted to talk with most often. Moreover, I knew what those little bright lights in her eyes were when she looked at me. They were the love-lights. And I usually found I had quite enough trouble with dames without having them in my hair in the very office where I worked.

I retrieved my hat from the waste-paper basket and opened the drawer of my desk to get at my store of cigarettes. The guy at the desk next to me, Charlie Lester, the political correspondent, leaned across and said: "The Chief's been looking for you, Hank."

"So I heard," I said shortly.

He grinned. "Don't look so sore. You may be getting a raise."

"Like to bet an even dollar?" I asked.

He shook his head wisely. "Do I look a mug?" he asked. Then he grimaced in pain. "My shoes are killing me," he complained, and bent down and loosened his laces.

14

The newsroom boy, Freckles as we called him, had been out on an errand. He entered just then. His eyes caught sight of me, and he came right over.

"Morning, Mr Janson," he said. It was only mid-morning, yet already he had managed to get ink on his fingers and forehead. His carroty hair stood up in spikes and his loosely-knotted tie had worked around to one side of his neck.

"Had your bath this morning, Freckles?"

"You know I have, Mr Janson. You ask me that every day."

"Is that so?" I grinned.

He leaned across the desk and said in a hoarse whisper: "The Chief wants you, Mr Janson. He's been asking everywhere for you."

"Okay, sonny," I chuckled. "Thanks for letting me in on it."

"That's okay," he said. "You can always rely on me to keep a check on things."

I grinned as he turned away, and winked at Lester. He grinned back. I got up. "Well," I said, "I'd better find out what it's all about."

I knuckled the frosted glass of the Chief's door, and pushed in without waiting for him to invite me. He never yelled "*come in*" anyway. If he had, he'd have been yelling "*come in*" a coupla thousand times a day. At times, his office was the most busy place in the whole building. Especially just before the paper went to bed.

He looked up from a pile of proofs he was blue-pencilling, and when he saw it was me, he flung down his pencil and leaned back in his chair. "I've been asking all over for you, Hank," he said.

"So I notice," I said. "I haven't yet had a chance to even visit the can."

The Chief was about fifty-five, powerfully built, hard-faced and grey haired. He had a bark that was like a wolf's howling for blood, and a bite that was short, sharp and decisive. But he rarely bit! He had been in the newspaper game all his life, and knew every angle. He demanded hard work from everybody, yet worked twice as hard himself. He was scrupulously fair and transparently honest. If you gave the Chief a square deal, he treated you like a son. In short, he was a hard, tough guy with a heart of gold. He was grand!

He leaned back in his chair, hooked his thumbs in his pant-suspenders and rolled his cigar from one corner of his mouth to the other. His clear, grey eyes looked straight at me as he said: "I got a new assignment for you."

15

I tensed all over and then made myself relax. "I'm working on an assignment right now," I said.

"I know. You'll have to drop it."

I stared at him. "Are you crazy?"

"You'll have to drop it," he repeated.

I looked at him, grinned, fished a pack of cigarettes from my pocket and sat on the corner of his desk as I lit up. "Okay, funny man," I said. "So you've had your joke. Now, what do you want to see me about?"

"I told you," he said seriously.

My jaw dropped. I looked at him closely, and I could see that he was serious.

"Listen, Chief," I said. "It's the big fight tonight. Remember? The birds are whispering that Kit Bronski has been boosted as a two to one winner. It's whispered that he's been told to take a dive. But Bronski's the kind of guy that fights while he's conscious. If Bronski doesn't take a dive tonight, a few guys will have lost a lotta dough. Losing dough will make them sore. Maybe they'll want to make Bronski sore as well. The cops have got the tip-off, and if anything breaks it will make one hell of a story."

"You teaching me to such eggs?" asked the Chief.

"Sorry," I apologised. "But it didn't seem you realised how important it is I should be there tonight."

"Conway will be there," the Chief said drily. "I've told Jenkins to handle the police angle."

I got mad all over. But I kept it inside me. No guy likes being taken off a job just like that. It makes him feel kinda cheap. Especially if he isn't consulted about it before it happens.

"Maybe you want yourself a new reporter," I said.

He eyed me steadily. "The way you're talking, Hank," he said, "it'll be you making that decision."

My anger began to seep out of me slowly. It seeped out in the form of hot words. "You don't want reporters. You want a lotta smart kids to push around just any way you want."

He got angry, too. His eyes flashed. "I want men who can do their job," he said loudly. "I don't want babies who cry for a lollipop when it's taken away from them. I want men who will do a job, whatever the job is."

"What the hell am I supposed to be?" I demanded hotly. "A robot, a pawn on a chess-board you can push around? You want yes-men, you have them! But I'm no yes-man and I won't be pushed around."

"You'll do what you're told," roared the Chief.

"I'll take no orders from you," I roared back. "I quit."

16

That was kinda final. He looked at me steadily and I glared back at him. The seconds ticked past as our temperatures slid back towards normal. He said quietly: "Okay, Hank. If that's the way you want it?"

"Yeah," I said. "That's the way I want it."

"I'll phone the pay-clerk to pay you for the rest of the month," he said quietly.

"Anything you say." I was beginning to feel sorry for what had happened. The Chief was a grand guy. He'd treated me swell. And my work on the *Chronicle* was my life, an integral part of me.

He said quietly: "It's a pity you got all that dough in the bank, Hank."

"What're you getting at?"

He shrugged his shoulders. "Having money does things to a fella sometimes," he said. "It kinda warps him. Take another fella who's got no dough in the bank and who's got to rely on his salary for his bread and butter. He'd act different, he'd really do his job. He wouldn't squawk like a scalded cat when he got a job that he didn't like. He'd have to take it for his bread and butter. But I guess having dough can make a difference in a fella. Anytime he doesn't like a job, he can chuck it in and live on his interest."

"You know that ain't true," I said hotly. "I'm not the kinda fella that gets clever because he's got money in the bank." His accusation stung deep.

"Looks that way to me," growled the Chief.

"Is zat so," I jeered. "Well, I can prove you wrong, Mr Clever Dick. Give me that assignment. I'll take it. I'll show you a thing or two."

"You don't want to quit no more?"

"Do you want me to take the job or don't you?" I grated.

"Okay, Hank," he shrugged. "You're back on the payroll." But there was a mischievous twinkle in his eye, and suddenly I realised he'd deliberately goaded me back on to the payroll and into taking this job. And because he was the kinda guy I liked, and because I wanted to be on the payroll anyway, I didn't argue. I liked it just the way it was.

"There's a seat reserved on the evening plane to St Louis," he said crisply. "You can get a bus or taxi from there to Benton, about twenty miles."

"What's the job?" I insisted.

He opened his desk drawer and pulled out a folded sheet of grubby writing paper. He handed it to me without a word. It was addressed from Benton and was written in a hand obviously unaccustomed to writing. The letter read:

> Mr Joe Healey, *Editor of* Chicago Chronicle.
> *Dear Sir,*
>   *Theys done got my grandson in thet durned rat-trap jail. Them say Johnny killed thet guy. But Johnny ain't ever murder nobody.*
>   *I knows for shore Johnny killed nobody. But thet durned Marshal ain't believing nobody, no-how. I'm an ole man now. Somebody's got fer to do sumthin' for Lanny 'cos I kan't do no more. I leeve it to you, afecshonally yours, Jake Peters.*

I read the letter through a second time, and then puckered my forehead. "This fella's crazy," I said.

"Maybe," said the Chief drily. "Maybe not. Go down there, Hank. Sort this thing out. Wade right in it up to your neck."

"I can't figure this out, Chief," I said. "There's liable to be all hell let loose at the fight tonight, and yet you want me to trail across country to a one-horse town, checking up on a two-bit murder for an old cracked guy."

The Chief's grey eyes bored into me. "I want you to do this job, Hank," he said. "I want you to give it your best. I'm asking you as Chief of the *Chronicle* and as a friend. What you say?"

There was an intensity and a sincerity about him that meant something special. I looked down at the letter I was still holding, and then looked back at him. "Okay, Chief," I said. "I still think it's screwy, but, I'll do my damnedest. If there's anything in it, I'll be right there in the midst of it, right up to my neck, just the way you want."

"That's fine, Hank," he said quietly, and for a moment there seemed to be a gleam of gratitude in his eyes.

"What about the plane reservations?" I asked.

"Miss Westhouse has got the ticket."

He scribbled on a memo sheet. "Better take this to the pay-clerk. That'll cover expenses while you're away."

I got as far as the door and had my hand on the door-handle when he said quietly: "I glad you took this job, Hank. It may be there's one more thing I ought to tell you now you have taken the job." He dropped his eyes to the desk blotter and toyed with his pencil. "Jake Peters' son was a buddy of mine twenty years ago. He was a good friend of mine. He was a good reporter, too. Thoroughly honest. So honest that he got dropped from a

18

speeding car right on the doorstep of his paper. There were so many slugs inside him, we didn't bother to count." He was silent for a moment, then added: "Anything I can do for his father or his son, I wanna do. Understand me, Hank?"

There was a lump in my throat as I realised now why the Chief had wanted me to undertake this job. He had a personal interest in it. But he had been loyal to the paper. Only when I was willing to work officially for the paper did he tell me about his personal interest.

"Leave it to me, Chief," I said. "Leave it to me."

There was still a lump in my throat when I closed the door behind me. He was a grand guy. A real grand guy.

CHAPTER TWO

I took the stairs to the floor above, to the *Woman's Page* section of the *Chronicle*. I walked along the corridor until I came to a door marked *Sheila Lang, Editress, Woman's Section*, and pushed inside.

It was more like a dame's boudoir than an office. There were chintz curtains at the windows, gaily-coloured armchairs and soft cushions, and vases of flowers placed in strategic positions.

"Hiya, scallywag!" I said.

"Hello, you big ape," she replied. "Why don't you learn to knock?"

She'd been adjusting her suspender when I came in. She dropped the hem of her skirt quickly and smoothed it along her thighs with her fingers.

"You've encouraged me never to knock," I told her.

"The way you act sometimes makes me think you've never seen a dame in your life."

I held my arms open wide. "Come. Give me a real big hello," I said.

A few minutes later she had pulled herself away and straightened her blouse. There was a flush on her cheeks and her eyes were sparkling. But she gave me a knowing look. "What's that for?" she demanded. "What's the bad news? I can take it."

I loosened my collar with my forefinger. "No fight tonight," I said. "I'm going out of town. I may be gone a few days."

"What?"

I nodded. "Special job."

She sighed and her eyes lost their sparkle. Me and Sheila had been pals for quite a while. She was a nice kid with a nice figure. She was small and compact, yet she had the energy of a dozen women; a real live-wire, concentrated dynamite! She had naturally curly hair that formed tight ringlets, and she wore a perpetually cheeky grin. She was the kind of dame any fella would have liked, and I wasn't any exception.

I figured Sheila perfect except for one thing. She was a wildcat when she was jealous, and she was jealous every time another dame got within a yard of me. And with a job like mine, when you're liable to rub shoulders with quite a lotta dames, me and Sheila tangled often.

"I've been looking forward all week to the fight," she pouted. That's the way it went with us. Most dates we made had to be broken on account of either of us being liable to go out on an assignment at short notice. Tonight should have been a cinch. We'd have been combining pleasure with work. But even that was broken off now.

"Where are you going?"

I told her all about it. She frowned and asked: "You don't know when you'll be back?"

"No idea."

She summoned up her cheeky smile and said: "Well, you can take me to lunch, anyway."

"Go powder your puss and make it snappy," I said.

When she got back, all powdered up and wearing a little hat and a smart coat, I eyed her with satisfaction. "You look like a million dollars, honey."

"Thanks. It's not often *you* pass compliments. But it's special today. I'm doing a fashion show this afternoon."

"You taking part in it?"

She grinned roguishly. "Just writing a coupla columns."

It was mid-way through the lunch when she got the bright idea.

"Hey, why don't you come over with me to the fashion show?"

"Naw," I drawled. "That's not my line. If it were a visit to the morgue, to visit a coupla stiffs or ..."

"Don't be so damned ghoulish," she snapped. "Everything's experience. Have you ever been to a fashion show?"

"No," I said. "Tell me, can I get myself a nice pair of underpants? Trimmed with lace and threaded with blue ribbon?"

"You'll find it a damned bore," she said. "But I'll be thrilled to bits. Jules Dupois is giving a special showing. There are sure to be some wonderful creations there."

"Who says I'm coming?" I grunted.

"I say," she flashed. "The way things are, we shan't have much chance to see each other for some time. Let's make the most of it while we can."

I shrugged. "Okay, scallywag. It's your party, though."

Apparently it was a very exclusive do. Only a few press tickets had been issued to the leading papers, and to carefully-selected buyers. The exhibition room was like a small theatre, with seats facing a small stage. A raised platform had been built up from the stage and along the centre aisle. This, I guessed, was for the models to walk along.

Sheila's ticket was for the front row, and I found myself sitting in the centre of the row with my shoulder nudging the raised platform. I looked around, and right away I could see this was no place for me. There were about forty or fifty folk there, and they were all dames. They weren't the friendly type of dames, either. They were the starched, prim, hoity-toity type. I eased around and looked at the old dame behind me. She was chin-deep in furs, as chesty as a penguin, smelt like a perfumery parlour and wore an ostrich feather in her hat about two feet long. She was sixty, trying to look like thirty. She still looked sixty. The powder was so thick on her face you could have scooped it off with a spoon. She had granite eyes and she used them on me. I don't like being looked at in that way. I stared back, equally hard.

She had one of those nasty looks that you carry in your hand. She raised those lorgnettes and stared through them at me. I know when I'm beaten. I gave up. I turned around and looked at the stage again.

Sheila said in a hushed, bored voice: "Jules Dupois is immensely clever, you know."

"Never heard of him."

"They rave about him," she said. "His touch is incredible."

"Has he been touching you that way?" I asked, suddenly aggressive.

"I'm referring to his artistic touch," she said coldly. "In many ways he's a genius." She broke off and nudged me with her elbow. "This is him," she said. She sounded like a bobby-soxer seeing Frank Sinatra for the first time. I looked up, expecting to see … that is, I don't know quite what I expected to see. But I certainly didn't expect to see what I did see. Jules Dupois was about five-six. He wore a beautifully-tailored morning dress, knife-edged trousers and a rose in his buttonhole. He had the hands of a woman and the face of a lily. His fair, golden hair was beautifully permed, and as he came onto the stage a cloud of perfume wafted across from him to me.

I screwed up my face, pinched my nose between my thumb and forefinger and said, "Ugh," loudly.

Sheila kicked me angrily, and Jules looked at me rather startled. I worked up a fixed grin, and he smirked back. The way he smirked made me feel sick. He was the kinda guy I wanted to punch in the puss at first sight.

He held up his hands in a gentle, feminine gesture, and he must have cut more ice there with the dames than Hitler did with the Gestapo. There was an immediate hushed, awed silence as those dames leaned forward in their seats, holding their breaths, waiting for the great Jules to speak.

He was also three parts actor. He stood poised there, one hand held delicately in the air, commanding silence, and his eyes staring dreamily over their heads. He held his audience that way for what must have been almost a minute.

Maybe he could get dames tied in a knot that way. But I wasn't a dame! I chose my moment carefully. I waited until he was about to tongue the eagerly-awaited words, and as his lips began to move, I cleared my throat loudly and went into a fit of coughing. Jules had made a wonderful entrance, but I guess I rather spoilt it for him.

He stared at me with a rather sad, pained expression in his eyes, waiting for me to finish. When I'd tucked my handkerchief away, he licked his lips and said: "Ladies," he licked his lips again, and then added with that pained expression on his face, "and gentleman."

All those dames were waiting with bated breath for what he had to say. I have to hand it to Jules. He sure could talk. He talked all the time about clothes. But he talked about them in a way I've never heard anybody talk about clothes before. He talked about the poetry of a dress. He compared it to a rhythm, music. He turned a blouse into an ode and an evening dress into a full symphony. He talked like a man inspired. His eyes flashed with the fire of inspiration, and his delicate hands fluttered like butterflies. My head whirled, and I listened in a kind of a dream, visualising women's clothes as something unreal, unsubstantial and like a vision. My mouth was dry, and I became conscious I was gaping like the village idiot. I was honest with myself. I hated Powder-Puff Billy on sight. But I had to admit that he sure could put it over.

He finished with a ringing falsetto trill: "And now. This season's models. My own creations."

He stepped to one side of the stage and made a magnificent gesture with his hand. The thick, golden cords pulled the heavy, black velvet curtains to one side and revealed, search-lighted in the centre of the small stage, a girl wearing a dazzling, sequin-covered evening dress.

The old dame behind leaned forward and jabbed me with her forefinger. "Please be so good as to remove your hat," she said coldly.

23

I turned around and mumbled an apology to her, conscious that all eyes were riveted upon me instead of upon the stage, and removed my hat. I looked around, wondering where I could put it, and finally plunked it down on the parade-aisle, which was level with my shoulder.

Jules must have been sensitive. He'd felt the temporary diversion of interest from his creation to my hat-removing activities. There was a sad look in his eyes as he gazed at me entreatingly. I winked at him and nodded, as much as to say: "*Carry on, fella. It's okay by me.*"

The model made a coupla turns, holding out the dress to show its full skirts, took a few mincing, swaying steps from one side of the stage to the other, and then began to walk the parade aisle. You could hear those dames all over the joint, sighing in ecstasy as though they were seeing something so wonderful that it took their breath away. I didn't see anything wonderful about it. It was just a dress. The model pirouetted slowly at the beginning of the parade aisle, and I caught her eyes looking at me meaningfully. I grinned back and said: "Hiya, toots."

The old dame gave a loud gasp of disgust. The air came out of her like she was a pricked balloon. Sheila's elbow gouged into me hard. Jules locked his fingers together like he was praying, and looked at me pathetically.

The model pirouetted again, slowly, her eyes catching mine meaningfully.

Sheila leaned over and whispered in my ear. "Hat," she said. "Hat!"

I got it then. I'd put my hat on the parade aisle. The model wanted me to move it. I reached for it quickly, too quickly, and knocked it over the far side. I sprawled half-way across the parade aisle trying to catch it. But I didn't quite make it. The spinsterish-looking dame whose lap it had fallen on, handed it back to me without a word. There was an icy tension everywhere. I could tell nobody liked me.

I sank back into my seat, put my hat on my lap and glanced at the model, who was coming out of her fourth pirouette. "Sorry about this," I muttered. "You can carry on now, toots."

The old dame behind me pricked her balloon again. Jules fluttered his eyes upwards to heaven, and Sheila gave me a savage kick in the ankle. The model's face remained serene and poised. But I thought I could see a smile quivering at the corners of her mouth.

She slowly paced the parade aisle to the far end, pirouetting every three paces while the onlookers voiced hushed, reverent comments of approval. When she came back and got near me, I saw Jules looking anxious. I could almost hear his sigh of relief when nothing untoward occurred.

The curtain went down on the model, and a few seconds later came up to show a second model. This one was wearing a black, sheath-like evening dress that fitted so tight around her thighs that she could take only six-inch steps. Sheila whispered fiercely in my ear: "If you ball this up, you big ape, I'll crucify you."

I didn't want to cause Sheila no trouble, so I sat there like a dormouse. I concentrated on keeping my hands and feet still. When the model walked the aisle, she pirouetted right by my shoulder. My eyes were on a level with her knees. She was so close I could see just how tightly that sheath-like dress fitted across her thighs. Sheila nudged me again, hard. I turned around and looked at her enquiringly.

"It's the dresses you're supposed to look at!" she said. She was getting good and jealous. She spoke louder than she'd intended. Everybody's eyes switched to us again, including Jules's. His eyes were pleading with us. Sheila blushed and looked at her feet. But it took more than a flock of hoity-toity dames to embarrass me. I turned back and went on looking at the model.

When the curtain came up on the fourth model, I didn't even see the dress. I just looked at the girl herself. And I recognised her! Somewhere among the hundreds of thousands of dames I'd cast eyes upon during my life, I musta run across this dame in some special kinda way. I remembered her well. The face was familiar. But I couldn't place it.

Her hair was so fair that it was almost white. It was parted on the right and hung down in one thick, shining wave to her shoulder, falling across her cheek and throwing that side of her face into shadows. She had steely blue eyes that seemed to glisten, and a sulky curve to her eyelids and eyelashes.

When she got level with me, I noticed the dress for the first time. It was black velvet, and no better model could have been chosen for the dress. And no better dress chosen for the model. She turned slowly, one hand on her hip and the other half-raised in the air. I caught her eye and gave her a broad wink. I saw a flicker of interest in her eyes, but no recognition.

I followed her closely as she walked the aisle, noticing every turn and twist of her body. It was only her face that was familiar. Some time, some place, I had seen her. It was like trying to remember a name I couldn't remember but was on the tip of my tongue. When she got back level with me again, I handed her another broad wink. Her forehead momentarily puckered in surprise. I was turned half-way around in my seat so I could wink at her without Sheila seeing. And that brought me almost face to face with the old crow behind. She let out another gasp when I winked, and handed another dirty look through her lorgnettes.

I turned around and sank down in my seat.

There were six dresses shown all told, and then Powder-Puff Billy gave another recitation. The one thing I gathered was that we were next to see some underclothes.

Sheila said doubtfully: "I thought this was just dresses."

"So what?" I said. "You're getting more than your money's worth."

"Maybe you didn't ought to be here," she said.

"A bit late to think of that now."

She looked at me calculatingly. "Don't you start getting any ideas, Mr Hank Janson. These girls are strictly models, no matter what they are wearing."

"Lay off," I said. "I didn't want to come in the first place." I fumbled in my pocket, got out a pack of cigarettes, stuck a cigarette in my mouth and began to light up as the curtain was raised for the first of the models. She was clad in a most enchanting two-piece set of undies.

Sheila jabbed hard with her elbow.

I knew she would be mad about me seeing dames in their undies. I said in a loud whisper: "I didn't want to come. You brought me here."

She said in a loud whisper: "You can't smoke here."

I could feel forty or fifty pairs of eyes boring into the back of my neck. Jules had that sad, pained look on his face again. I took the cigarette from my mouth and put it back into the pack just as Sheila nudged me hard again. She nudged hard enough to knock my cigarettes to the floor.

I swore softly and bent down to pick them up. My hat was in my way, so I put that up on the parade aisle and went down on my knees.

When I climbed up into my seat again, the tip-up seat squealed as I lowered myself into it. Jules was looking at me as if he thought I might explode like a bomb any minute.

"Nice dame," I said to Sheila.

The model had reached the beginning of the parade aisle. She turned slowly, took two paces, which brought her just in front of me, and turned again slowly. The panties were tailored, and fitted over her hips with a tantalizing emphasis. The short legs of the panties were wide. Very wide! Her legs were long and shapely and her skin was smooth and soft, and I figured that when she was right level with me I'd be able to see ...

Sheila nudged me hard with her elbow and attempted to distract my attention. Or so I thought. Jules was looking at me again now with his hands clasped appealingly. His eyes were shining, as though filled with unshed, pleading tears. The old crow behind drew in a harsh, rasping breath, and I felt the eyes of everybody fastened upon me. What did I care? I had come there to see, hadn't I?

I switched my eyes back to the model. As I had thought, now she was right level with me, I could see all the way up her thighs, right to the hip, and as she turned ...

I suddenly realised what the tension was about. My hat was on the parade aisle again. I made a quick, sudden snatch, and almost brought the house down. The model had been closer to my hat than she had thought, and her high-heeled shoe was on the brim of it. When I snatched my hat, I pulled her leg away from underneath her.

She gave a gasp, and so did every other dame there. She lurched as she swung her arms wildly, trying to recover her balance. Instinctively I tried to save her, and placed the flat of my palm hard against her buttocks to prevent her staggering over backwards. I saved her. She recovered her balance.

Did I say she had wide legs to those panties? My reactions had been instinctively to save the girl. I did save her. But I hadn't time to figure out all the angles, and my hand went up the inside of those panties instead of the outside.

You should have heard the squawks that went up then! The old crow behind nearly blew her front teeth out, she gasped so hard. I snatched my hand down quickly and tried to look like butter wouldn't melt in my mouth. But I could still feel the warmth of her body tingling on my fingers. The model was imbued with the good old "*on with the show*" spirit, and carried on without a falter. Her poise and self-assurance carried off what could have been an unpleasant incident. She paced along towards the end of the parade and I shot a look at Jules. Great tears were welling slowly down his cheeks. He looked like a man for whom the whole world is finished. Sheila hissed fiercely in my ear: "We're getting out of here."

"You go," I said. "I like it here."

"We're getting out," she repeated.

"You can go," I said. "I'll stay."

27

"I'll make you sorry for this, you big ape," she said. "I'm not leaving you here alone. I'm staying too."

"You should have brought some peanuts," I said.

She stamped on my foot hard with her sharp heel, and I moaned aloud. Jules looked at me so pleadingly that my heart almost broke.

When the fair-haired dame came out again – the one whose name I couldn't remember – I gave her another broad wink. Her eyes rested on me momentarily. They were laughing eyes, trying to laugh for me alone, and to present to the rest of the assembly a cold indifference. I ventured another broad wink, taking care that lorgnettes behind me should not catch it.

I'd been too busy catching her eye to take note of what she was wearing, until she began the return trip along the aisle. She was wearing wide-legged panties, too, and when she turned slowly a little way from me, I inclined my head and caught a glimpse of her shapely thighs disappearing into subtle shadows. Unthinkingly, I gave a low whistle, and immediately the place became charged with an electric, hostile atmosphere. The girl's cheeks coloured faintly and her eyes went hard. Jules wrung his hands in misery and even I, tough as I am, was chilled by the icy hostility of all those frigid dames staring at me.

I sank down low in my chair and tried to make out I wasn't there. But that was difficult, because Sheila was fiercely pinching my thigh black and blue. And she was saying harsh, fierce things to me beneath her breath.

After that, I took great care to keep things on a level keel. The rest of the undies were exhibited with only careful side-looks from me, to enliven the exhibition.

I watched the nightdress parade with lingering, longing eyes, and decided without a doubt that the nightdress model I would like to have in bed beside me was the fair-headed dame. Her eyes didn't glance at me. If they had, they'd have been contemptuous. I kept racking my brains, wondering where I had seen her before.

There was a showing of shawls, of cute hats, and, to me, a surprising item: six exhibits of what were known as "falsies." They didn't use the fair-headed girl to demonstrate these. They called in a coupla flat-chested dames they musta got special for the job.

After that, Powder-Puff Billy gave a talk on the importance of foundation garments, and the models did their stuff again, showing just how unromantic foundations could make their young bodies look.

All this time, Jules had not stopped being acutely conscious of my presence. Every time a new model made her entrance, Jules shot me a side-long glance of apprehension. But as nothing further untoward occurred to upset the tranquillity of his artistic showing, he became less jumpy and more confident of himself.

The fair-headed dame showed off a garment he called a *Nude-Lastique-Sheath*. As corsets go, it wasn't too bad. It lived up to its title, too, which gave me plenty to think about and got Sheila fidgety. But it must have been darned uncomfortable to wear, just the same. The fair-headed dame had slim thighs. Yet that corset fitted so tight that, even on her, a roll of skin formed where the corset ended.

"The next item," announced Jules, "will be a special modern model of the old type lace-up corsets for the Modern Miss." It had, he explained, daring contours and was suitable for all outsize ladies. To demonstrate this, he was using an outsize model. The outsize model sure was outsize! Only the guys behind the scenes know how they managed to pack her into that corset. Her generous chest was cramped into the constricting garment, and you could see the sickly grin of suffocation on her face. Where the garment ended, her meaty thighs swelled like balloons.

Jules overplayed his hand. He explained that this particular garment combined grace with an ability to mould the body firmly. The Modern Miss, he added, was easy to operate. To add weight to this statement, he invited one of his other models onto the stage to demonstrate how easily the corset could be unlaced.

The outsize dame stood sideways to the audience, while the other model, keeping a firm hand on the ribbons, unlaced three or four inches. You should have seen the look of relief on the fat dame's face as she sucked in a few useful breaths. Having demonstrated the point, the model then began to lace up again. But maybe the fat dame's deep breathing had spoiled things. The corsets wouldn't meet at the back. The lacer strained, but the edges wouldn't come even. Everybody leaned forward in their seats, tensed, watching. Jules fidgeted. The lacer took a deep breath and renewed her efforts. The fat woman looked pained, but the corsets still didn't meet. Jules grinned weakly at the audience, and said: "Sometimes the last of the lacing requires a little extra effort."

He said something aside to the lacer, and she rested her knee against the fat woman's broad buttocks and applied more pressure. She still didn't get anywhere, and Jules was now patently agitated. His agitation affected the lacer. She took another deep breath and tugged savagely. The fat dame had been holding

29

her breath, trying to accommodate the lacer. She couldn't hold her breath any longer and let it out with a loud "Ah-ahhr." She did this at the same time as the lacer tugged hard. Two things happened simultaneously. One of the lacing ribbons snapped at the same time as the outsized dame breathed out. It looked rather like Carnera * snapping a thin ribbon tied around his forearms by flexing his muscles. The lacing at the back of the corsets came undone like it was a zip being pulled down, and the fat dame fell out of the corset. I say fell out. But that's an understatement. She had big, generous breasts, and they practically cascaded out of the gaping and loose corset. I'd been trying to be good. But this was too much. I rocked with laughter. Sheila could have jabbed me with her elbow, the dame behind could have looked at me through her lorgnettes, and the rest of the dames could have tried to freeze me with hostile glances, but it would have had no effect upon me. I just had to laugh and I did laugh. You'd have laughed, too, if you'd seen it. I still rocked with laughter as they let down the curtains and blacked out the embarrassed outsize dame, the worried lacer and the distracted Jules.

But nobody else thought it funny. All those dames stared at me in stony silence as I wiped my eyes. It did something to me. It got me cowed. I didn't think it was funny any more. I shut up and once more hunched myself in my seat. If you ever burst right out laughing to yourself in a crowded subway train, and everybody turns and looks at you in surprise, you'll know just the way I felt then.

It was a merciful relief for me when Jules appeared in front of the curtain once more and attracted everybody's attention away from me. He was a broken man. But he was game. He was going on with the show. His face was damp with perspiration. His delicate hands no longer fluttered like a butterfly: they quivered with apprehension! He gave me a long, sad, pained, soulful look and, as though pleading with me, announced that the next exhibit was to be the last. And this exhibit was his finest creation. Its value and ingenuity, he went on, would be the sensation of the world.

The he gave a lot more spiel about it. I guess that guy must have had poetry in his soul. He compared his new creation to

---

* Footnote to the Telos edition: Primo Carnera, a former boxer and wrestler, was well-known for his strong-man act when the first edition of *Some Look Better Dead* was published.

30

the universe. He pointed out that the sun with its surrounding planets, including the Earth and Moon, were but a single constellation. If from a distance, he went on, you looked at the sun and its planets and yet another sun and its planets and yet even another sun and its planets, and if the distance was enough, you would see these mighty constellations as but one star. One single star! And a dozen of these single stars, he continued, if viewed from a sufficiently distant point, would themselves make up but one single star.

I didn't know where all this was getting to. I vaguely wondered if he had been reading H G Wells. He went on talking glibly about the Earth being composed of layer upon layer of different soils until it finally made up a total world as we know it.

Personally I thought it was all hooey. But the rest of the dames were leaning forward in rapt attention. They clung to every word he let drop, as though it was a thousand dollar bill. It was a hell of a long speech, and he wrapped it all up with quotations and poetry. Mentally I shrugged my shoulders. After all, if he could make his bread and butter talking to dames that way, who was I to bawl him out?

He finished his speech at last and announced in high dramatic tones: "And now. My own special creation, which I call The Five Veils."

He bowed and the curtain swept back, showing my model, the fair-headed girl, wearing his creation. I guess I don't know much about dames' clothes, but even I could tell this was something special. The dame looked like she was wearing a kinda blue mist. She was dressed, but there was a slinky, subtle suggestion of transparency about the dress. When I examined it carefully, I could see that it was some kinda filmy, transparent net. It was as though her warm, white body moved like a shadow beneath the dress.

Jules took the fair-haired girl's hand, and led her on to the beginning of the parade aisle. She stood there, poised for the moment, and then revolved slowly. She looked ravishing!

"This," said Jules proudly, "is 'The Evening Dress'."

I could tell it was an evening dress, because it was ankle length. It had long balloon sleeves that gathered at the cuffs, and through it, her arms looked like a blue mist. From her knees down, too, I could see her legs as clearly as though I was seeing them through the finest of veils. From the knees upwards, the dress, in a way that I couldn't understand, seemed to conceal yet reveal her limbs.

31

"And now," said Jules in a ringing voice, "'The Tea-Dress' – away with veil number five!" As he spoke, he began to unbutton something at her back, so that the top covering of blue net slid away in his hands. He'd taken it off like he would take off an apron, and now the fair-haired girl revolved once more, slowly, only this time the blue mist ended at her knees instead of her ankles, and she was wearing a tantalizingly intimate tea dress.

I began to get something then on Jules's build-up about layer and layer. He had been talking about this dress. I settled down to watch in earnest and, judging from the sighs of pleasure I heard from all around me, the rest of the party liked it as well.

Jules purred with satisfaction. The second veil slipped, he said, to reveal the most enchanting of under-slips.

He did some more unbuttoning, and this time a lot more net came away. It left the model standing in a blue under-slip that finished about three inches above her knees. As she poised and turned slowly, her skin gleamed through the blue mist. Through the under-slip I could see clearly the outlines of a transparent brassiere and panties. But by some subtlety, the deepest mystery of her beauty eluded me.

The model had completed her turn, and again Jules was purring loudly with satisfaction at the ecstatic sighs and applause from his audience. He smiled, opened his mouth to speak, and then suddenly his eyes caught mine. He hesitated. That haunted look returned to his eyes and he hesitated for a moment. But then he took a hold on himself, worked up a smile, and said: "The third veil drops to show the finest and most subtle of two-piece undergarments."

He helped the model to pull the slip over her head, and there she was, clad only in exhilarating, misty blue, transparent panties and brassiere through which her flesh gleamed like alabaster. I feasted my eyes on her. I caressed her from head to toe, but mostly from shoulder to thigh. Those kind of clothes would have been exciting on anyone. On this dame they were especially exciting. I leaned forward, and Jules looked at me imploringly. The dame was still turning slowly. As she came around facing me again, my eyes automatically sought her three points of interest. And I was astonished, because her body was still able to make some slight, subtle evasion of my hungry eyes.

Jules looked at me pleadingly, fidgeted uncertainly and then, as though making the decision to trust to luck, made his last announcement.

"The fourth veil slips, ladies and gentlemen, in order to reveal to you the inner subtlety of this creation."

I believe that up to now the fair-headed girl had been so engrossed in her work that she'd forgotten about me. Not once had she looked at me. But now she tensed all over and looked down at me sharply. Her eyes met mine. Hard, hostile eyes, challenging, defying and contemptuous. There was a message to read in her eyes if I wanted to. It was a simple message: "*Get to hell outta here.*"

I grinned, treated her to another of my broad winks and leaned back comfortably in my chair. She tossed her head and looked at the back of the theatre, a fixed smile on her face.

Jules looked at me with desperation, licked his lips nervously and took one of the fair dame's hands and led her back to the centre of the stage.

Then he made a great effort, smiled calmly and said: "The fourth veil slips."

He ducked around the model, unbuttoned the brassiere, and quickly jerked her panties down around her thighs. So quickly did he do this that the brassiere had still not fallen clear of her breasts as he straightened up.

The subtlety of the elusiveness of her sweeter beauty was startlingly revealed beneath the strong arc lamps. A single blue strand around her breasts, as slender as twine, supported two haloes of transparent net about the size of a dime. These circles covered but did not conceal the twin points of my interest.

And then my eyes glided down over the soft, warm flesh of her belly, to where another slender blue thread around her loins supported an insignificant triangle of the same transparent material.

That dame was a dream of enchantment. All my innermost emotions fused into one pinpoint of desire, and I too for the first time let loose a long, ecstatic sigh of awe and admiration.

Those dames had been doing that every time they saw a dress they liked. But the way they all looked at me and bristled, you'd have thought I'd committed murder or something.

Powder-Puff Billy heard my ecstatic sigh and sensed danger in the atmosphere. I saw his face begin to blanch as, in sudden desperation, he snapped his fingers loudly, forestalling any further disasters. At this signal, the arc lamps snapped off and the black velvet curtains fell softly into place.

That was the end of the show.

Jules was waiting at the exit to shake hands with everybody before they left. Sheila's face was hard and set in grim rage. She had made me sit there until everybody had left, all the time

33

telling me what a beast I was for ogling women the way I did and for making a public nuisance of myself.

When we reached the exit, Jules shook hands with Sheila and eyed me nervously.

"You enjoyed my show?" he asked politely.

"It sure was hot stuff," I said. "Do you use live models all the time?"

"Why, naturally," he said. "How else could I fit ...?"

"How much will you charge to teach me the trade?" I asked.

His eyes widened and his mouth dropped open. "Teach you the trade ...?" he began, flabbergasted.

"He's kidding," said Sheila savagely. "He's a great kidder." She looked at me hard and gave me a surreptitious kick on the ankle.

"I see. A joke," said Jules. He gave a sickly grin. "Yes, a joke."

"Any time you're putting on that dance of the five veils again," I told him, "you can count me in for a ticket."

His face went white and perspiration sprang out of his forehead. "Excuse me, please," he said. "May I enquire? Are you a press representative or trade?"

"Press," I said.

He swallowed something in his throat, put his hands over his heart and croaked: "Will you ... that is .... are you likely to come ... I mean, will you be in regular attendance ...?"

I broke in on him. "Don't worry, buddy," I told him, "you won't see me around any more fashion shows. It's not my line of country."

I've never seen such relief shining in a man's eyes before. I'm certain if I hadn't been there he would have sunk down on his knees and extended his hands to the heavens thanking the gods for his rescue from imminent danger.

Sheila took me by the arm. "Let's get out of here," she said. She smiled a farewell to Jules, and I gave him my familiar broad wink. He beamed after us like a man who's been reprieved from a life-long sentence in Alcatraz.

Sheila started in on me as soon as we got outside. It was a monologue. She clung to my arm and skipped along beside me, taking two paces to my one. And all the time, she called me all the big dumb apes and lustful ogres that she could think of.

"And twice," she said with emphasis. "Twice you put your hat on the parade aisle."

I'd been trying not to hear her. When I could, I was thinking about the fair-headed dame. And then, when she reached this point, the words she uttered echoed in my mind again and again. "Twice," she said. "Twice you put your hat on the parade aisle."

"Twice! Twice! Twice!"

I snapped my fingers. "Stop. Stop it," I said.

"Stop what?"

"The girl's name," I said. "Trice, Fay Trice. Now I remember."

She stopped stock still, disentangling her arm from mine, and said slowly: "What Fay? What Trice? What dame are you talking about now?" Her voice was like ice-chips.

I was already in a jam with Sheila. I wasn't going to get in any deeper. I grabbed her by the arm and urged her along the street.

"Just like you said, Sheila," I said. "I put my hat on the parade aisle – twice."

"Are you screwy or something?" she asked.

"I feel like a damp rag after that exhibition. Let's grab a cup of coffee and simmer down."

"Huh, you've got to simmer down, have you?" she said with an angry glint in her eyes.

"Coffee," I said quickly, and urged her forcibly into the entrance of a drug store.

CHAPTER THREE

It wasn't surprising that I hadn't remembered the fair-haired girl's name until Sheila had prodded my memory with her comment. Thinking back, I realise it must have been almost five years since I'd first seen Fay Trice. And then I'd seen her only once more after that. What really was surprising perhaps was that I remembered her at all, after that length of time.

But the circumstances under which I first met her were memorable!

It started when I was in the station precincts over on West side. I was a cub reporter then, and had draped myself across the Inspector's desk while I told him what a clever fella I was. That was so he'd remember to ring me if anything really interesting broke.

A plain-clothes dick entered, and said to the Inspector: "We've got a search warrant for the Trice joint. Do you want to come on over with us?"

The Inspector began to climb into his jacket. "Maybe something to get our teeth into now," he muttered.

"What's this?" I asked quickly.

The dick drawled softly: "Just a check up, fella; just a check up."

"What about it, Inspector?" I asked. "Can I come along?"

He looked at me doubtfully. "Aw, I don't know. Maybe it'll come to nothing."

"It won't hurt to have me around," I said slyly.

He looked at me ponderingly. "All right," he agreed at last. "You can sit in on it. But no news, no story. Understand?"

"Sure, that's okay, Inspector."

I travelled with the Inspector and the dick in one car, and another car followed behind carrying four more plain-clothes men. On the way, I got the facts out of the Inspector.

There are still a number of big houses over on West side that sit well back off the road, surrounded by large gardens. Edward Trice, a stockbroker, owned one such house. Six months earlier, a change had entered Trice's life. A big house like his needed many servants. But the servants had all been dismissed, even the chauffeur. Trice continued living in the house by himself, leaving for the office in the morning and coming straight home every evening.

And at the same time that the servants had been dismissed, Trice's wife had completely disappeared. Not one glimpse of her had been seen by anyone in the neighbourhood. And Trice himself had become uncommunicative. He ignored his neighbours, spoke to no-one.

And as time passed, the neighbours became suspicious. The tradesmen who had delivered food to the house began to talk. Neighbours began to talk. Quite a lotta talk started all round. And, as usually happens in such circumstances, one of the neighbours finally wound up at the station, voicing his fears that Trice had done away with his wife.

The cops are used to that kinda complaint. They get a dozen like it every week. If nosey neighbours had their way, half the husbands in America would be picked up on a murder rap because their wives have taken a long vacation or gone home to Mother.

But, even so, the cops have to undertake a routine investigation, just because of the one guy in a hundred thousand who does bump off his wife.

A plain-clothes dick had made a routine call at Trice's house. He hadn't let on he was a dick. He'd said Fay was an old friend of his wife's, and he wanted to trace her. Trice had shrugged his shoulders, said his wife had left him and the last he had heard of her had been from California three months earlier, where she was stopping with her sister.

The information had accordingly been sent to the Los Angeles police, and wheels had turned slowly, and in the course of time a report had come back that there was no trace of Fay Trice at the address given, nor had there ever been.

That was when the Inspector had applied for the search warrant.

"You think he may have killed his wife?" I asked anxiously.

The Inspector shrugged. "It's happened before. There's plenty of ground at the back of the house, too. I wonder how many of these guys do it and get away with it?"

We rolled up the drive to the house and parked outside the door. Me, the Inspector and the dick walked up to the front door. Those in the other car remained there. The Inspector rang the bell, and after a long wait the door was opened. The dick flashed his badge and pushed inside. The Inspector followed, and I crowded behind.

It was a big house, dark and gloomy and dusty with neglect. It could have been a nice house, but right then it was badly in need of attention.

The Inspector said solemnly: "Are you Edward Trice?"

Trice licked his lips. "Yeah, that's right," he said nervously. I looked him over, impressing him on my mind. He was an average man; average height, average width of shoulders and average bulk. His hair was thick and black and plastered down on his head on either side of the central straight and wide parting. His face was hard and white, his mouth generous but mostly compressed into a slit, and his eyelids were heavy, so that most of the time his black eyes seemed to be hooded.

The Inspector flashed a paper. "That's an order to search the joint," he said.

Trice was obviously agitated. "I don't understand," he faltered. "I don't understand what this is about."

"We'll talk about that later," the Inspector said crisply. He jerked his head at the dick, who went outside and came in with the other four men.

"Just sit down, will you, Mr Trice?" said the Inspector.

Trice clenched his fingers into two hard fists, looked like he was going to say something, and then thought better of it. He sat down in a chair, and sat there gnawing his fingernails while he watched us furtively.

"Just keep an eye on him, Jenkins," instructed the Inspector. Then he instructed the others to go to the upper rooms, and he himself chose the rear of the house. The dick I had travelled with had been instructed to search the basement. Because the basement seemed to me to be the place where a wrong guy might plant his deceased everloving, I tagged along with the dick.

As soon as we opened the door leading down to the basement, we were hit by the smell. And as we walked down the steps, it surrounded us like an invisible cloud; the unbearable, filthy stench of a pig-sty.

"Should have brought a gas-mask for this job," commented the dick sourly.

"What's he got down here, pigs?" I asked.

"We'll find out," he said grimly.

We switched the light on at the foot of the stairs, and it was lucky we did so. The basement corridor was paved with stone, and evil-smelling liquid puddled the low-lying places.

"Let's get outta here," I said.

"That's okay for you," said the dick. "But I've got a job to do."

A number of doors lined the corridor. But the end door attracted our attention immediately. It was heavily bolted, and at the base

38

of it, on floor level, was a tiny hatchway. It was from this hatchway that the smell seemed to be emanating.

The dick took his handkerchief from his pocket and clapped it over his nostrils. I followed suit. He picked his way carefully over to the door, and hammered on it. I don't know what he expected to hear, but there came a rustle of movement from inside, rather like that of an animal changing position. The dick gave me a startled look, shot back the bolts, and dragged the door open.

That was when I first saw Fay Trice. She was alive. But what kind of living could that be?

Her hair and body were so matted with filth that we didn't realise at first that she was completely naked. Her eyes were closed and she whimpered insanely and groped at us with taloned fingers as though she was blind.

Getting her out of there was one of the most distasteful jobs I'd ever undergone. Me and the dick did it between us. And after we'd got her upstairs and she'd been sent off somewhere and Trice had been taken off to the lock-up, I steamed myself in a Turkish bath for six hours and still didn't feel clean.

Well, that's how I first met Fay Trice. Very unusual circumstances! And nobody'd ever be satisfied if I leave it at that, so I'll put in a few more details.

Like most of these things, you can never get the true story. But subsequently I got all sides of the story and, lumping it all together and trying to be impartial, this is roughly an account of what did happen.

That Eddie and Fay Trice were in love with each other there is no doubt. It was a violent and passionate love, with inflamed jealousy playing a large part on either side. Eddie, a successful young man, carried on a stockbroker's office, completely single-handed, desiring neither to split his profits with a partner nor to allow others to assume part of the burden of his work. At business he was a quiet, reserved, thoughtful type of man, but, as is often the case, at home he was a tyrant. He treated his wife brutally. Servants testified freely to this, and Eddie did not deny it. But, as is often the case with women who love passionately, his brutality was a spur to her love. Although her face frequently bore the marks of his fist, nothing could erase the loving devotion in her eyes whenever she looked at him.

At some time, Eddie became suspicious of Fay's loyalty. She claims these suspicions were unjustified. Be that as it may, Eddie watched her as a cat watches a mouse, and his uncontrolled jealousy induced him to make plans. There came a day when

Eddie returned home from his office early and discovered Fay in her negligee with a young man.

The real truth of this is in dispute. Fay asserts that she had just finished bathing when the young man called to service the vacuum cleaner. Yet it was significant that this was the day all the staff had off!

Eddie, inflamed beyond measure, asked for no explanation. He must have been in a killing mood. The young man was knocked down three times before he flung himself bodily through the French windows at the back of the house in a desperate, and fortunately successful, attempt to escape.

Still Eddie asked no explanation. He turned his attention to Fay. He ripped off her negligee, and when she attempted to resist him, he stretched her on the floor with a savage punch. As, dazed, she staggered to her feet, he ripped the rest of her underclothing from her, leaving her as naked as the day she was born. Once more he hit out at her, and as she lay moaning on the ground, he seized her by the hair and dragged her across the room and down the basement steps. Her body was bruised and torn by every one of the rough wooden stairs.

At the far end of the corridor was a small cupboard, about two feet deep and three feet wide. It was possible to stand upright in this cupboard or to sit down, cramped up with the knees under the chin. But it was impossible therein to stretch out and rest. It was into this cupboard that Fay was bundled to sob over her injuries and to reflect upon what had happened.

The cupboard was unlighted and the darkness thick, like a blanket. At first Fay waited for release, but then, as the hours passed and she heard no sound and saw nothing except the eternal blackness, she became filled with panic. Her cramped muscles would not stand the strain for long of sitting with her knees hunched beneath her chin. And when she stood hour after hour, her legs and ankles began to ache with the strain of it. The floor was of wood and the walls were of stone. Her tender, naked skin was chaffed and torn. Fortunately, because of the time of year, she was not unpleasantly cold.

For a few hours, she restrained her impulse to batter at the door, knowing it would do her no good. But as the hours crawled past and her discomfort increased, she became desperate. She hammered at the door, shouted, tried to attract Eddie's attention, and the only answer she got was the echo of her voice.

Many hours later, cramped and pained beyond belief, half-crazed with panic, and with the pain of hunger clawing at her belly, her eyes, now accustomed to total blackness, were painfully seared by a faint glimmer of light beneath the door. Her heart beat rapidly as she heard footsteps approaching and she realised she was about to be released.

But never had she been so mistaken before. Eddie had been preparing his plans of revenge for a long while. There was a little hatch at the foot of the door. This hatch, when opened, enabled him to slide through two bowls, one of water and the other of food.

She yelled, pummelled at the door, screamed, pleaded with him and tried every way she knew how to reason with him. But Eddie was merciless. The hatch clicked shut, was strongly bolted and the footsteps retreated along the corridor, and darkness came down upon her again.

Not for another twenty-four hours did she hear from Eddie again, and that was when he brought her two more bowls of food and water. And these bowls he did not slide in to her until she had returned the other two. And for the next six months, the only communion Fay had with any living soul was when Eddie supplied her with food every twenty-four hours, and not once during that whole six months did Eddie speak a word to her.

Imagine the plight of that poor girl? Imagine her feelings as the days passed slowly, her intense bodily discomfort, her fear of losing her eyesight because of the perpetual surrounding darkness, and the horrifying torment in a naturally clean girl of her unhygienic conditions.

She never saw the water she drank and she never saw the food she ate. Maybe that was just as well. Everything she ate was a boiled, pulpy mess. And we afterwards discovered that Eddie had a large saucepan into which he put all his waste and boiled it, rather as a farmer will boil pig-swill.

How long passed before Fay decided to bring an end to this intolerable existence is not known. If she bore this for a week before deciding to end her life, it would have been a long while. But when she finally made the decision, she then realised how carefully Eddie had planned all this. The clothing with which she might have slowly and painfully strangled herself, he'd taken from her. The two bowls that were her perpetual companions were of rubber! It seemed that Eddie had thought of everything. There was one thing that Eddie had not thought of, however, and you could not expect him to have done so. Only a girl in the desperate position that Faye found herself would even have thought of such a means to finish her life. Her fingernails grew. Even Eddie couldn't stop that happening. And as her fingernails grew longer, so Fay sharpened them to a sharp edge against the stone wall. When they were sharp enough, Fay tried to dig for her pulse. She never succeeded, but when she was taken to hospital, her wrists were torn and jagged in a dozen places.

Eddie made a plea of insanity and was examined by mental specialists and deemed to be in full possession of his intelligence. He was given a sentence of up to five years' imprisonment. Fay was too ill to appear in the courtroom, but dictated all the details of her complaint against him to police representatives. It was reported that she was obsessed by an overwhelming desire to cause him to suffer as she had suffered. Divorce proceedings were instituted immediately.

I saw Fay Trice once more after that. I paid a visit to the hospital. She was resting, but the nurse allowed me to creep in and see her for a moment. She was sleeping like a child, with her fair hair splayed out over the pillows. Her face was gaunt and there were deep black rings around her eyes. But, just the same, I could see the beauty that must have been hers.

All that had been five years ago, and now I had seen Fay Trice for the third time, and seeing her I knew that she had recovered fully from what must have been one of the most terrible experiences ever suffered by a woman.

CHAPTER FOUR

Sheila dropped me off from her taxi at the airport and went on to a cocktail party held by a firm of face-cream manufacturers.

I had half an hour to spare, so I spent it sipping a whisky at the bar. When the microphone announced my plane was due to depart, I finished my drink and sauntered out onto the tarmac.

It was a twenty-four seater Constellation, and all the seats were numbered according to the tickets. The seats on the left-hand side were in pairs, and my seat was the outside one. I would have preferred the inside, because it was easier to look through the window. I've travelled by plane many times, but I've never got over the minor thrill one gets when the plane first leaves the ground and swoops high in the air, and one sees the aerodrome and the countryside diminishing into what looks like a child's toy farmyard.

The seats filled up quickly, but the one next to me remained vacant. I glanced around. All the seats were now filled. The air-hostess was talking to a steward and checking through her passenger list. It looked like we were waiting for just one passenger. I began to feel that perhaps after all I might get the window seat.

The hostess fidgeted for another ten minutes, and then a decision seemed to be reached. An authoritative voice said: "Can't wait any longer." But almost immediately afterwards, another voice called from the outside: "Hold it a minute. Here's somebody."

It was somebody. Everybody craned their necks around as the late passenger climbed breathless into the machine. I was the only one who didn't stop staring at her. Because right away I saw she was the fair-headed model I'd seen that same afternoon. And right away I knew that she was going to sit right next to me.

The air-hostess led her down to the seat, and I got up and stood on one side so she could climb in. She was so breathless and confused that she didn't even glance at me. When she began to wedge her attache case into the rack, I reached out and said: "Allow me."

She looked at me then. Her eyes widened in surprise, and then hardened into annoyance. Instinctively she glanced around.

43

"Hard luck, lady," I said. "You're stuck with me. No other seats available."

She looked at me coldly and sat down. She didn't say anything. I tucked the attache case away carefully and then sat down beside her. "Remember me?" I asked conversationally. "I was at the show this afternoon. The cat in among the pigeons, remember?"

"The analogy is not quite right," she corrected me. "The wolf who demanded his pound of flesh would be more appropriate." She flushed slightly, and I knew she was remembering the way I had stuck to my seat when the fourth veil was slipped.

"I learned one thing," I said. "It isn't the clothes that make the woman. It's the woman that makes the clothes."

She stared at me stonily, and then very pointedly looked out through the window. I sighed, and just then the air-hostess requested that we fasten our belts.

I let it ride after that. The doors were closed and the plane taxied into position. I watched the pilot revving up the alternate engines, getting them warm, and then he gave the engines the gun.

The plane had plenty of acceleration, and when the tail went up and the floor inside the plane levelled off, the seat pressed hard against my back. Then there was that moment of exhilaration as the wheels left the ground and all at once we were in the air, climbing rapidly and turning slowly as the ground dropped ever and more rapidly away from us. The plane went on climbing until it entered the clouds, passed through them and levelled out above.

Beneath us, the clouds stretched out like huge white blankets, and the plane seemed motionless. It would stay that way, I knew, until we reached St Louis, where the plane would climb down through the clouds to the landing field.

We had loosened our safety belts, and the fair-headed dame reached for her attache case. She opened it and began to take out a book. The initials on the attache case were L D.

"You've got the wrong case," I said.

"I beg your pardon," she said coldly.

"Anyhow," I amended, "you've got the wrong initials."

"I don't think so at all," she said. "What do you think they should be?"

"How about F T?" I said. "That stands for Fay Trice."

That got her. She gave me a long, hard stare, then said: "What do you know about Fay Trice?" Her voice was cold, unfriendly.

44

"I was there when they got her out of the cellar," I said. "I helped carry her up the stairs."

"You were there!" she said.

"Yeah, I was there. She wouldn't remember me, though. I saw her only that time and one other when I visited her at the hospital."

"What were you doing in that house?"

"Reporter," I said.

Her eyes widened with understanding. "You must be Hank Janson," she said.

"Fancy remembering the name."

"Naturally I would," she said.

"I must compliment you on having made a miraculous recovery from what must have been a terrible ordeal."

She raised her eyebrows. "Me?"

"Who else?"

Then she chuckled. "You're getting me confused, Mr Janson. Many people have made the same mistake. Fay is my sister."

"Your sister," I echoed. Then, rather foolishly, I added: "Then your name isn't Fay Trice?"

"No," she said. "It's Lynn. Lynn Darwin. Darwin was Fay's maiden name too."

"So you're not married?" I said.

She gave me a saucy sideways glance from beneath lowered eyelids. "That sounds like a leading question."

"I've got lots of them," I said. "Are you stopping in St Louis? Are you working there? Do you like bacon and eggs for breakfast? How do you like your men, tall or dark?"

"Such an inquisitive little man!" she said.

"Not so inquisitive," I said. "After all, we're acquainted in a kinda way. I knew your sister and I've met you before, too."

She flushed again, prettily. "If you don't mind," she said, "I'd like to forget this afternoon. I had no idea there would be any men present when I took the job. I wouldn't have carried on either, except that it would have broken Jules's heart."

"Okay," I said cheerily, "skip this afternoon. What about this evening? What are you doing in St Louis?"

"There's no reason why you shouldn't know," she said. "I'm going to see Fay."

"She's well?"

Her face clouded. "She hasn't been too well."

"Married again?" I asked.

45

"You wouldn't have heard about it," she said, "but after the court case, Fay had a relapse. She'd undergone a severe mental strain. She was very seriously upset for a time."

I said quietly: "There's an asylum in St Louis."

"There's no reason why you shouldn't know," she said quietly. "But she's made great progress during the past year. And today is a kind of red letter day, really. She's well enough to come out. They've made me her guardian."

I thought that over. "That's pretty tough on a working girl."

She smiled. "It's not so bad. Mother left me a little money when she died. I've got enough for us to live on for a year or so, and Fay will be better by then. I've taken a bungalow for the season at Benton. And, anyway, I've earned myself a good rest."

"Don't kid me," I said. "You don't kill yourself just walking around modelling clothes."

"Don't kid yourself," she retorted. "It's damned hard work. I've done three shows a day sometimes. Each of them fifty miles apart, and every time I've had to take off and put on as many as twenty or thirty dresses."

"That shouldn't kill you," I sneered.

"It would kill you," she snapped. "Why, last week I showed about twenty pairs of corsets in one afternoon. They were all new, never been stretched before, and by the time I was through, I was pinched black and blue all over ..." She broke off as she saw the grin on my face, and blushed again. "Look, don't let's get back on that subject again," she said quickly.

"This place, Benton," I said casually. "Why do you pick that?"

"Plenty of reasons. It's on the Mississippi, there's plenty of swimming and the sun, it's near St Louis if ever ..." She didn't finish that sentence. "... And Fay herself knows Benton. She'd like to stop there."

"You've picked the right place," I said.

"In what way?"

"Benton," I said slowly, "is the place I'm going to."

"Perhaps you'll look me up," she said.

"That," I said slowly, "was just what I was hoping you'd say." I gave her a special kind of look. She stared back at me for a moment, and then her eyes dropped shyly. "It will be nice to see you," she said.

"That too," I said, "was what I was hoping you would say."

CHAPTER FIVE

When we landed as St Louis Airport, me and Lynn split up.

She'd made all her plans. She was picking Fay up from the asylum and had booked a hackney carriage that would take her straight to her bungalow in Benton.

As for me, I had a job to do anyway.

It was about twenty miles to Benton. I caught a bus just outside the airport, and an hour later it dropped me off at a small, typical mid-west town. It was a quiet kinda place. You could see that here everything ran smoothly but slowly. There was little to do and plenty of time to do it. Nobody hurried, nobody hustled, and if you lived here, you could take your time growing old.

I booked myself a room at one of the three hotels that Benton possessed, and cleaned myself up. Then, although it was evening, I decided to poke around a bit.

The reception clerk informed me that the Marshal's office was just along the street, and I went there on the off-chance there was some information I could pick up.

The Marshal's office was a newly-built, white stone block that was also the County Hall as well as tax collection and other civil administrative offices.

Much to my surprise, the Marshal himself was still at the office, although it was well into the evening. I presented my credentials and was conveyed along a corridor to an office marked with the words:

CLEVE SANDERS – MARSHAL

"Take a seat," said Sanders, and, as I did so, the clerk who'd accompanied me obeyed the quick glance that Sanders flashed at him and went out quietly, closing the door behind him.

I looked across the desk and eyed Sanders keenly. He was a big-built man, about fifty years of age; his thinning hair was still black except for the grey tufts above his ears. He had a ponderous air with him, as though he was constantly chewing and digesting everything he heard, and everything he was about to say. His necktie was loose, the shirt he was wearing bore sweat stains under the arm-pits, and a worn, baggy tweed jacket hung over the back of his chair. He looked me over, looked down at my credentials, which were spread out in front of him, and frowned.

"Long way off your beat, aren't you, Janson?"

"News anywhere in America concerns the *Chronicle*," I said.

He gave me a sharp look. "How come you're so interested in Johnny Peters?"

"You know how it is," I said. "Anything for a story."

He gathered up my papers quickly, shuffled them together and handed them across the desk to me. "This is a legal office," he said. "We're not here to supply newspapers with their news."

"Mr Sanders," I said quietly. "I'm not wanting a sob-story. I'm wanting facts. You can give me those facts. On the other hand, you can refuse them. Either way, it makes little difference to me." I leaned forward across the desk. "I can get all the facts I want. It may take me longer, but I'll get them just the same. But maybe it wouldn't look so good in the paper, to say how I didn't get co-operation from the Marshal."

He eyed me steadily. "You ain't threatening me, are you, son?"

"I'm not threatening," I said. "I'm just out after facts. It's my job to get them."

He looked at me hard, looked at the calendar on the wall behind me, switched his eyes to his desk drawer, dived his hand in and pulled out a box of cigars. "Smoke?"

"I prefer cigarettes," I told him, and got out my pack.

He examined the cigar as though he had never seen it before, drew it along beneath his nostrils, and bit off the end. He spat the end with unerring accuracy two yards across the room, where it scored a target in a big brass cuspidor. "What do you want to know?" he asked, without looking at me and applying a match to the end of the cigar.

"Give me an outline of what you know about the whole business," I asked.

He drew steadily at the cigar until it was well alight, leaned back in his chair with his hands clasped together in front of him, and spoke to the ceiling.

"The man who's been murdered," he said quietly, "is Ellis Tundall. He worked upstairs, in the Treasury Department. I'll give you the facts as we know them, and you can draw your own conclusion."

He paused for a moment while his eyes seemed to examine the ceiling with minute care. Then he went on: "One lunch hour, Tundall sent one of his assistants down to the bank to draw some money from his own personal account. It was a lotta

48

dough. Five hundred bucks. The assistant brought back the dough, and there were four fellas in the office who saw Tundall put the money in his wallet. Shortly afterwards, Tundall went out. He said where he was going. His car was at Johnny Peters' garage, where it'd been for four days undergoing repairs. He was off to get his car."

He paused again. A long pause. "That was the last anybody saw of Tundall. He walked out of this office like that, and never came back.

"Four days passed before the folk here began wondering what could have happened to him. The fellas in his office came down to see me. I sent a man over to Johnny Peters' garage. Johnny Peters hadn't seen him either. Johnny claimed he had received a phoney telephone call for a breakdown. He had taken his breakdown wagon twenty-five miles out, only to find it was a hoax. Johnny claimed he hadn't been near his garage that day."

"Can you check this?" I asked.

"We tried," he said sharply. "It didn't get us anywhere."

"Sorry to interrupt."

He nodded. "That's okay." Then he went on. "Another two days passed, and the folks in the Treasury Department began to put pressure on me. Just for the hell of it, I sent a man out to Johnny's place again. Johnny wasn't around, and my man poked around a bit. Maybe he was exceeding his duties. Up until he made the discovery, that is. He found the dollar bills under a loose floor board in Johnny's workshop. There was an axe wrapped up in canvas lying beside it. The axe was bloodstained, and human hairs were adhering to it."

"Circumstantial evidence only," I said.

He lowered his eyes, looked at me steadily and then looked at the ceiling again. "We brought Johnny Peters down the jail for questioning. He's an awkward boy to deal with. Pretty hot-headed. We didn't get anywhere with the questioning, except Johnny denied any knowledge of the money or the axe."

"The money really did belong to Tundall?" I asked.

"Sure," he said. "We checked on that. The bank had the numbers of the notes Tundall had drawn. They were the same."

"You're building up quite a case against Johnny Peters," I said.

"It gets stronger," he said. "So far we hadn't got a body. You can't do much when you haven't got a body. We wanted to prove whose blood was on the axe. We wanted to prove whose hair. But we still hadn't got a body."

"Your boys are so smart and find so much, maybe they could borrow a body," I said.

Again his eyes came down from the ceiling and rested on me steadily. He could have got flaming mad. But he didn't. All he said, softly, was: "This department doesn't work that way, son."

"Okay," I said. "Give me the body angle. Where did you find it?"

"My men were around his garage for another four days before they found it. They were looking for evidence of burial or dismembering or burning. They didn't see what was right under their noses. It wasn't until the fourth day that one of my smart boys realised that a vat of hydrochloric acid is one way of disposing of a body."

I sat forward in my chair. There was a cold shudder running down my spine.

"We ran off the acid," he continued calmly. "I don't know if you are aware of it, Janson, but platinum and gold are about the only things apart from glass that hydrochloric acid will not dissolve."

I nodded. "I've been to school."

"We found a platinum watch medallion and a gold ring. Both of these were identified as being the property of Tundall."

"Nothing else left?"

For a moment there was a pained pucker on his forehead. "There was something else," he admitted. "At the bottom of the vat was a whole pile of sludge. The kind of residue that would be left after hydrochloric acid got to work on flesh and bones."

I felt slightly sick. "What does Johnny Peters say about all this?"

"Denies everything."

"What about Tundall? Who was he? What do you know about him?"

He brought his eyes down from the ceiling and levelled them at me. He leaned forward with his elbows on the desk. "I've been twenty years at this game," he said. "I've checked all angles. I've checked on Tundall, too. He was a good man, did his job well in the Treasury Department, and earned himself a good salary. There's been no complaint yet about his work at all. But there must have been wheels within wheels working with the administration. He must have known somebody who could pull strings. Tundall got his job here without any references. Nothing is known of him before the very moment he arrived in Benton three years ago."

"What does he look like?"

"There is not one photograph of him that can be found. He lived in a hotel and possessed only the few necessities of life such as a toothbrush, suit, towels and so on."

"You reckon Johnny Peters killed Tundall?" I asked.

He looked at me steadily. "What do you think?" he said. "What do you think the jury will say?"

I stood up. "Thanks for the information, Marshal. And if you are still holding Peters, what's the chance of seeing him?"

"We've got him down the jail. He's charged. It's a charge that looks like it's going to stick."

"What's the chance of seeing him?" I repeated gruffly.

He looked doubtful. "He's a tough kid to get along with," he said.

I said fiercely: "Do I get to see him or not?"

He shrugged his shoulders. "You can see him," he said mildly.

One of his assistants escorted me down the road to the county jail, and in the meantime the Marshal telephoned through, instructing them to allow me to see Peters.

A cop swinging a large key-ring escorted me along the corridor to Peters' cell.

"He's a tough one, this guy," said the cop. He shuddered. "What a thing to do to a dead guy," he added.

I grunted. I didn't like cops who shot off their mouths.

We reached the door of Johnny's cell and I said to the cop: "You can lock me in with him for a while. I'll shout when I want out."

He chuckled grimly. "It's your funeral, fella," he said.

He opened the iron grille and I stepped inside. He slammed it shut behind me and locked it again. I waited until the footsteps had echoed away down the corridor, and then said quietly: "Hiya, Johnny."

He was a young, earnest-looking kid, sitting on his bunk and looking at me with hatred in his eyes.

He didn't move, he didn't speak, and I felt the hostility emanating from him like an evil cloud. I fished in my pocket for a cigarette pack and offered him one.

He ignored it.

I shrugged my shoulders, put a cigarette between my lips and lit up. "About this murder," I said.

He was like greased lightning. He moved so quickly that I didn't even know he had begun to move until his fist connected with my jaw and my head slammed back against the hard iron

51

grille behind me. For a moment I saw stars. I shook my head, trying to clear it, fingered my jaw tentatively and looked at him through dazed eyes.

He was standing there, trembling with range, his hands bunched into hard fists and his eyes blazing. "Say that again, fella," he said ominously. "Just say it again. How many more guys have I gotta sock for saying that?"

He was small and tough, but I could have handled him with ease. But I wasn't in that cell in order to beat him to a pulp. I fingered my lip, which was split, and dabbed at it with my handkerchief. "What makes you so tough?" I asked.

"Say it again," he warned. "Just say it again."

"I'm from the *Chicago Chronicle*," I said. When I announce the name *Chicago Chronicle*, folks usually stare at me in awe and expect miracles to happen. Johnny wasn't made that way.

He said: "I don't care where in hell you come from."

"I wanna talk with you, Johnny," I said seriously.

"I ain't in a talking mood," he said. "Just start in on that murder business again and see what happens."

I sighed. There was nothing I could do. He was just fighting mad. I raised my voice and yelled for the guard. He let me out and locked the door carefully behind me. He grinned when he saw me dabbing at my lip.

"That fella sure is tough," he said. "You're the seventh guy he's taken a sock at."

"What's he so touchy about?"

The cop shrugged. "Seems kinda sensitive. Every time somebody starts talking about murder he just sees red and lams out."

"I wonder how he'll get on when he's in court?"

The cop chuckled deeply. "The law's on our side," he said. "We can chain him down if we want."

I got outside, still dabbing my split lip, and a bulky figure detached itself from the shadows and loomed alongside me.

"Have a drink, Janson?" said a familiar voice. It was Cleve Sanders, the Marshal.

I looked at him doubtfully. "Waiting for information?" I asked.

"Come and have a drink," he said.

We went into a bar and climbed up on the high stools. He didn't ask me what I wanted, but he ordered two bourbons.

"How'd you get on?" he asked.

I dabbed my lip and showed him my blood-flecked handkerchief. He nodded understandingly. His eyes were tired and weary.

"What do you make of it?" he asked.

I gave him a sharp, sidelong glance and picked up my glass and sipped. I deliberately ignored his question.

He understood. He said: "I'm a cop, Janson. I've been on the force for twenty years, but when I walk out of that office, I'm off duty. I'm off duty now. I'm talking to you man to man."

"A cop's on duty; on or off," I retorted.

"Officially," agreed Sanders. "But not here," and he touched his heart.

"What are you getting at?" I demanded.

"You've seen Johnny Peters," he said. "Does he act like a guilty guy to you? It gets him flaming mad that anybody should even suspect him of murder."

"Are you rowing for the other team in your off time?" I asked sarcastically.

"Don't get me wrong, Janson," he said. "I've known that boy since he was at school. He ain't the kinda kid to bump off somebody for a few measly bucks. I've got my job to do, and the chips are stacked against Johnny Peters. But if there is anything that can be done to save that boy, count me in."

I looked at him, and he stared right back at me. And right away I knew he was sincere. I could sense, too, his internal conflict. His job and the evidence against Johnny Peters were taking him in one direction, and Clive Sanders was hating like hell the path he was being forced to tread.

I reached out my hand and took his. "I'll remember that," I said. "Maybe you can help me sometime."

"I hope so," he said seriously. The he asked, casually: "Have you seen the boy's father yet?"

"Jake Peters?"

He nodded. "You ought to see him."

"I aim to," I told him. "It was Jake Peters' letter that brought me down here."

"Jake Peters told me something," he said. "I checked on it as hard as I knew how. It didn't get me no place. I wish it could have done." He sighed and took another sip at his drink. "Jake's an old fella," he added. "You can't rely on anything he says no more, and you've got to bear in mind that Johnny is his grandson."

"I'll see Jake," I said.

He finished his drink and stood up. "Don't forget, Janson," he said. "Any time I can do anything."

"I'll remember," I told him.

* * *

53

Jake Peters was an eccentric. He was of the generation whose fathers had rolled wagons across the prairie, fighting off attacking Indians.

He lived in an old shack a coupla miles out of town, cooked for himself on an open stove and used oil lamps. When he heard I was from the *Chronicle* he went crazy with delight.

He produced a bottle of rot-gut and two dusty glasses and we sat opposite each other at his rickety wooden table.

"You know something about this murder," I said, coming straight to the point. "What is it you know?"

"I can prove Johnny ain't kilt that man, and this is how I know it."

He told me something, and my heart jumped. For a moment I thought everything from now on would be easy, but then I suddenly remembered Cleve Sanders' remarks.

"Are you sure of this?"

"Sure I'm sure," said Jake. "But that Marshal and them durned legal folk all think I'm crazy." He tittered. The old boy looked a little crazy to me. And Cleve Sanders had assured me that he had checked this angle as far as he could and had got nowhere.

"How well did you know Tundall?" I asked.

His sharp eyes flicked at me artfully. "I knowed him durned well," he said. "Every day I seed him at the County Hall."

"How come you saw him every day?"

"I worked there," he said proudly. "I'm the door keeper." He tittered again. "That's why folks think I'm crazy. I've got lots of dough in the bank but I don't spend it. I save it. And I like living in this shack. And I like my work."

"You're getting on, Jake," I said. "Why do you want to go on working?"

He tittered again, rolled his eyes artfully and said: "Standing up there on the County steps I see life. I see folks coming and going. And it's like the whole of America passing along in front of me so that I can watch them and think about them."

"Where does that get you?" I asked.

He chuckled, drained off his drink, and said artfully: "I'm a philosopher, son. I guess one way of finding out about life is to find out about your fellow men."

He gave me an uneasy feeling. He could know what he was talking about, but, like the Marshal had said, he was getting a little old, and maybe a little crazy at that.

54

"What are you gonna do with all that dough you got?" I asked.

He looked at me hard, got up suddenly from the table and walked across to the stove. Then, in sudden anger, he swung his arm in an arc and smashed his glass on the floor. "It was for my grandson," he said angrily. "If those durned legal varmints would listen to sense, he wouldn't be locked up there in that jail."

He looked like he was working himself into a fit of temper. I said, quietly but insistently, jerking him back to the present: "Why did Johnny have a vat of hydrochloric acid at the garage?"

He came across to the table again. He looked at me artfully. "That's a good question," he said. "Nobody's thought of asking that."

I looked at him in amazement. "You mean, nobody's asked that question before?"

He leaned forward and said slowly: "No. Nobody's asked that question before. And d'you know why, son? Because everybody knew why he had that vat there!" He went off into a peal of laughter, and he slapped me on the shoulders. A cold shudder ran down my spine.

"Why was it there?" I insisted, after he had stopped laughing.

He looked suddenly serious. "My Johnny's a clever boy," he said. "Everybody knew that the garage wasn't making money. He worked it single-handed, and even then there wasn't enough work for him. But he was a clever boy. He was inventing, see. He was working on a new method of galvanizing sheet metal." He gave me a quick, bird-like glance. "D'you know what that means, son?"

I nodded. "I get it," I said. "Hydrochloric acid is used to clean sheet metal before it's galvanized."

He nodded eagerly. "That's a good answer, isn't it, son?"

There wasn't much more I could get out of Jake. I swallowed another glass of his rot-gut and got out as quickly as I could.

I went back to my hotel and climbed into bed, reckoning that I'd had a really busy day. And I knew that the next morning I'd be able to look at everything I'd learned in a new light. I'd get nowhere mulling it over in my mind right then.

CHAPTER SIX

The next morning I rang the Chief.

"How are you making out?" he asked.

"Not too good," I told him. "Johnny Peters looks like he's for the high jump."

His voice was serious, almost hurt. "Nothing we can do?"

"You know me," I said. "Anything I can do, I will."

"What did Jake Peters have to say?"

"You seen him recently?"

"Not in twenty years."

"Don't get me wrong, Chief," I said. "But twenty years is a long time."

"What are you getting at?"

"He's a nice old fella," I said. "But everybody has to get old, I guess. He didn't have much to say."

"What was his angle?"

I told the Chief what Jake Peters had told me. He thought it over and said: "That's good enough, Hank. Work on it."

"You don't get it, Chief," I protested. "Jake Peters is as crazy as a coot. Why, the way he acted last night, I wouldn't have been surprised to find him in a nut-house."

"I suppose he kept bursting into fits of laughter?" said the Chief.

"That's right." I was slightly surprised.

"Then he shot off his mouth about philosophy and about looking at people and about how it made him think about life."

"Maybe there was a microphone under the table."

He laughed. "Jake Peters ain't changed," he said. "He's a bit eccentric, maybe, and he gets wild ideas. But he ain't changed. He always was that way."

"Sounded real crazy to me."

"It always did when people met him for the first time. When they'd known him a while, they altered their minds. And if that's what Jake Peters told you, you can rely on it that it's the straight goods."

"You want me to follow up a bum steer like that?" I demanded.

"You haven't any other lead?"

"No," I said. "That's the only lead I've got."

"Work on it, Hank," he said earnestly. "If that's what Jake Peters said, there's something in it."

I thought that over. "It looks like I'd better just hang around and wait for things to break."

"Something's sure to break."

"Okay," I said. "I'll hang around. And since it's a waiting game, you can get busy on the legal side, getting the prosecution bothered. Get a coupla writs for *habeas corpus* issued."

"Two writs?" he queried.

"Yeah," I drawled. "One writ to produce the body of Johnny Peters, and deliver him from jail, and the other writ," I chuckled and added, "for the production of the body of Ellis Tundall."

"I'll get busy on that," he promised. "Keep in touch."

Well, there it was. I just had to play a waiting game. I had time on my hands. And having time on my hands and the memory of a Five Veil dress creation lingering at the back of my mind meant just one thing.

I checked out of the hotel, fixed up with a garage for the hire of a sedan for a week and asked directions to the address Lynn Darwin had given me.

When I tried to start the car, it seemed like the plugs weren't sparking. I scowled at the garage man and he grinned back at me. "This ain't gonna give no trouble, I hope," I said.

He winked at me, reached into the car and fingered something under the dashboard. "Try again," he said.

The engine purred into life. I scowled. "What's this, a box of tricks?"

"Secret cut-out," he said. "Use it, buddy. Coupla years ago there was an epidemic of car-snatching. We had all our cars fitted with that cut-out."

"I'll remember to fit one on mine," I said. "That car's really worth stealing."

Lynn Darwin's bungalow was a coupla miles out of town. I drove along a second class road alongside the Mississippi and located her bungalow about half a mile from the nearest habitation. It was a small, compact bungalow with a drive-in and a private foreshore to the river. I swung up the drive, parked the car so it wouldn't be in the way of the blue sports model parked in the garage, and operated my secret cut-out.

I got no answer when I knocked at the door, so I went around the house, along a narrow, gravelled path and found myself at the back of the house. It was a good day, the sun was shining fine, and Lynn and a girl who looked very much like her, and who I realised must be Fay, were sunning themselves in swimming costumes on the bank of the river.

I walked down the lawn towards them, and Lynn heard me coming and jumped to her feet quickly. "So pleased you've come, Hank," she said. She was talking quickly as though wanting to talk me down. "I want you to meet my sister, Fay. Fay, this is Hank. Mr Hank Travers. You've never met him before."

There was a warning in her eyes, and I caught on. The last time I'd met Fay, she'd just undergone a terrible ordeal. There was no point in reminding her of it. I placidly accepted the name Travers that Lynn had given me.

I could see right away that Fay was entirely different from Lynn. If I hadn't known, I'd never have guessed at her history. Neither at her enforced imprisonment or her convalescence in the asylum. She was gay and vivacious, cheeky and sly, and full of life. Her first comment was, as she looked me over approvingly: "My, my, I never thought Lynn could make such a good pick-up."

"Me and Lynn are old friends," I said. I eased myself down onto the ground beside her. Fay looked me over again. "Quite a man," she grinned.

Lynn looked embarrassed. She said quickly: "Don't get wrong ideas, Fay. Me and Hank are old friends. That's all. Just old friends."

Fay gave a down-and-under look from beneath her eyelashes that seemed to say, "*Who are you kidding*," and then looked back at me approvingly. "Any friend of Lynn's is a friend of mine," she said. She worked an awful significance into her voice.

Lynn didn't like the turn the conversation was taking. "Did you bring your costume, Hank?" she asked, changing the subject quickly.

I exhibited the bundle under my arm.

"Come up to the house. You can change there."

She led the way and I followed. Fay hastily climbed to her feet and strung along with us. I looked her over. I looked Lynn over. They were both wearing white satin swimming costumes. They were one-piece costumes, but only just. They were cut away front, back and sides so severely that they were more revealing that a two-piece costume would be.

"Not frightened of getting sunburnt?" I asked Lynn.

"Looking forward to it," she said. "I shan't be working for at least six months. So I can have a healthy brown tan instead of the white skin necessary for modelling evening dresses."

"You model swimming costumes almost as well."

She frowned at me in warning. She didn't want me to say anything smart-alec in front of Fay.

As I said, the bungalow was small and compact. There was a big living room that opened off on to the lawn through wide French windows. At the rear of the living room and side by side were a bedroom and a kitchen. You had to pass through the bedroom to reach the bathroom.

Lynn showed me into the bedroom and left me to it. I stripped off my shorts, shirt and pants and climbed into my swim-shorts. When I went back down the lawn, they were both lying stretched out in the sun, looking like lazy cats enjoying the warmth.

Fay sat up and looked at me cheekily. Her eyes wandered over my body approvingly, and I got some idea of just how a dame can feel when she is being sized up by a guy who wants to make her.

Lynn saw the way she was looking at me and said: "If you want to swim, Hank, don't wait for us. We've had our dip."

"Think I will," I said. I was beginning to feel uncomfortable.

There was a springboard jutting out from the bank. I bounced up and down on it a few times, testing it out, and then took a header. The river at this point was good and wide. I swam lazily, rejoicing in the cool caress of the water over my limbs. I swam out a long way and floated on my back, feeling the sun beating down on me, then lazily rolled in the water before I swam back again.

Fay swam out to meet me, her long, fair hair spread out on the water behind her. When she got close she yelled: "Open your legs. I'm going to dive through them."

I trod water, and then floated, keeping my head above water by moving my hands and keeping my legs astride. Fay looked at me, gauged the distance, seal-dived and disappeared beneath the water. I looked down through the water and, after a second or two, saw her blurred figure swimming towards me with an easy grace. A coupla yards away, she extended her arms, kicked out hard and glided between my legs, her body rolling over on her back as she did so. Her side brushed against the inside of my thigh, and then she broke water behind me. I turned around, and she demanded breathlessly: "Can you do that?"

"Shouldn't be surprised."

"Okay. Try it."

She swam a good distance from me, turned around and waved. "Okay. I'm waiting for you."

I dived, pulled myself down and along underneath the water and kept my eyes open. Fay had been quite a way from me when I dived. It seemed like I'd been swimming ages before I caught sight of the blurred outline of her outstretched legs. I changed direction slightly and swam towards her. When she was close enough, I extended my hands and kicked hard with my legs. I shot through the water, my lungs bursting, thankful that within a second or two I should be gasping for air. With my shoulders half through her legs, I rolled over on my back. I'd just made the turn and was squarely beneath her when she suddenly dropped down on me. She sat on my chest, and immediately her legs locked around me and gripped me tight. Instead of shooting to the surface and breaking water, I found myself sinking down with her weight on top of me. I hadn't been reckoning on anything like this, and my lungs were nearly bursting. I tried to wriggle myself free, but her legs clamped around me even tighter. We kept sinking! I couldn't hold my breath another second. The blood was hammering in my temples and I knew a moment of panic. I grabbed hold of her waist and tried to pull myself free. She clung like a limpet. I could almost picture her giggling about it. It was okay for her. She hadn't been underwater all the time I had.

I had to do something desperate. I did it. I reached out, grabbed hold of a piece of her, pinched it between finger and thumb and twisted real hard. She let go then. I plummeted to the surface, thinking I'd never make it, and thankfully breathed in the good, fresh air when my head broke through the surface. A second later, she bobbed up a yard or so from me. "Hey, you goof," she yelled. "You hurt me." But she didn't sound really annoyed.

I'd had enough of this. Without a word, I turned around and struck out for the bank. She yelled something after me. I didn't take any notice. When I reached the bank and pulled myself out, she was floating on her back, idling in the sun, apparently without a care on her mind.

Lynn smiled quietly. "Thanks for backing me up, Mr Travers."

"That's okay," I said. I jerked my head towards Fay. "She ought to be tied down."

"Why?"

"Too lively."

"How?"

"Skip it," I said.

There was a pause. Then she asked, thoughtfully: "What do you think of her?"

"A dame that lively. I'd say she was okay."

60

"I'm worried, Hank," she confessed. "You know the way it is. She's under my care. I'm responsible for her. If anything should go wrong, she'd have to go back to St Louis."

I detected the note of worry in her voice. "What's the trouble?" I asked. "You can tell me."

"She's got a mind of her own," said Lynn. "Last night, she tried to leave here. I didn't know she was going. But I heard the car engine and got to her before she could back out of the garage."

"Where was she going?"

"I don't know," she confessed. "Just anywhere, I guess. She's been penned up for all these years, and I guess she just feels she wants to be really free."

"If she's made up her mind to leave you," I pointed out, "you're going to have your work cut out preventing her."

"I've got the car keys locked away," she said, "and I've got all her clothes locked up. She can't get far without clothes. Maybe in two or three days she'll settle down."

"Must be pretty worrying."

"It is," she agreed. Lynn looked good and worried. "So many years she's been at St Louis," she went on. "I don't really know her now. She's changed in many ways." She turned and looked at me pleadingly. "Could you stay here tonight, Hank?" she said. "I'm worried. Fay seems desperately anxious to get away. She might try anything ..."

When she looked at me like that, with soft, appealing eyes, there was nothing I could refuse her. "Sure," I said. "I'll stop tonight. I'll be around." I gently patted her bare shoulder, and she flinched back from my fingers as though they were red-hot. She blushed, and her eyes dropped. Then, as though mutely apologising, she edged a little closer to me, until her shoulder was touching mine. It was like a kinda electrical tension. I said, wondering at the dryness of my voice: "Let's go up to the house and grab a drink."

Fay was treading water and calling out to us. "Come on in," she cried. "It's lovely. Come on in."

Lynn looked at Fay and then looked back at me. "Better not, Hank," she said. "Better not. Later, perhaps."

We stayed out as long as the sun. We picnicked on the lawn, splitting a chicken and a bottle of champagne between us, and it was a lazy, pleasant and drowsy day. Towards evening, as the sun set, we went on up to the house. Fay switched on the radio and began waltzing with herself, humming the words in a low, husky voice. She seemed quite happy. Lynn disappeared into her bedroom and came out some minutes later looking very cool and trim in the check-print frock she'd changed into. "Want to change, Hank?" she asked.

I went into the bedroom and changed back into my clothes. When I came out, Lynn was in the kitchen with an apron around her, preparing a meal. Fay was trying to find another station.

I sat in a chair and smoked a cigarette, while I watched Fay, bending over the radio. Dressed as she was in a swimming costume, I could see just how she compared with Lynn. She too would have made a good model, I guessed.

The sun dropped lower, and as dusk descended it became more difficult to see. Fay switched on the light and went off to the bedroom to change.

A coupla minutes later she was back, wearing an ankle-length dressing gown drawn together by a cord. Immediately she came out, I knew she was good and mad. She said loudly: "Lynn. How dare you!"

Lynn came out from the kitchen with that worried look in her eyes. As she wiped her hands on her apron, she asked soothingly: "What's the matter, Fay?"

"You've locked my clothes away," said Fay. Her face was flushed with temper.

Lynn said quietly: "I left something out for you."

"I want my clothes," said Fay firmly and loudly.

"Don't let's go through all that again, darling," said Lynn pacifically. "You won't be needing them anyway. We're not going out tonight."

Fay looked at me, and I could see she was angered and humiliated. "I won't have it," she said, and stamped her foot.

"I'm sorry, but that's the way it is," said Lynn firmly. She turned as though to go back into the kitchen.

"Wait a minute," said Fay. Her voice had taken on a hard, mocking tone.

Lynn waited. Fay looked at her intently, and then she looked at me with a half-smile curling her lips. There was a sudden, subtle change in her manner. "So you won't let me have my clothes?" she asked.

"Don't let's talk about it any more."

"If that's the way you want it, Lynn," Fay said, "you can't blame me for what happens." She looked in my direction, smiled deliberately and provokingly, and walked across and stood in front of me. "My sister won't let me have my clothes, Hank," she said. There was a husky, tantalizing note in her voice.

"I guess she knows best."

"Well, if my sister wants me around that way in front of her fella, that's her look-out, I guess!" said Fay. She sent a side-long glance towards Lynn. At the same moment, she untied the cord of her girdle and with a quick movement shook the wrap back over her shoulders so it slipped down around her ankles. All she wore beneath the wrap was a pair of white briefs. They had elastic at the waist and around the legs. They fitted very tight, and they were very, very brief. The looked like a pair of bloomers many sizes too small.

Lynn gave a sharp, sudden cry of protest that sounded like a cry of pain. "Fay," she cried. "How can you? How can you do such a thing?"

Fay stood squarely in front of me with her hands on her hips. She moved her boy slowly and sensuously, and smiled archly. "Do you like me better than my sister, Hank?" she cooed.

"Fay," screamed Lynn. "Stop that this minute!"

"It was your idea, Lynn," said Fay. "If you won't let me have my clothes, what else can I do?" Her tone was mocking, and she felt confident she had the upper hand.

"You'll get cold, Fay," I said. "Why don't you put your wrap on again?"

"I'm not cold," purred Fay. Without moving, she seemed to thrust herself closer to me. Her breasts were hard and pointed and creamy-white.

"What can I do?" asked Lynn despairingly.

"She's not cold," I said mildly. "If that is the way she wants it, why worry?"

Lynn said: "I don't know how you can do it, Fay. I hope you come to your senses pretty soon." She made as though to turn back into the kitchen.

I saw Fay's eyes narrow angrily. "Wait a minute Lynn," she said. Her voice was ugly.

"Well?" said Lynn wearily.

"Pretty sure of your grip on your boyfriend, aren't you?" leered Fay.

"We're just good friends," said Lynn.

Fay's eyes flashed angrily. "Do I get my clothes?" she demanded.

"We'll talk about it later," said Lynn.

"All right, sister," said Fay grimly. "How do you think your boyfriend will like this!"

Fay looked at me and smiled provocatively. "How about having me for your girlfriend?" she asked winningly. As she spoke, she thrust her body towards me and began to roll her briefs down over her hips.

Her movements were slow and deliberate, but so unexpected that the garment was half-way down her hips before Lynn screamed out, "Stop!" in a horrified voice.

Fay stopped. Only just in time. Her briefs were rolled down into a straight line across her thighs. I could see the full, soft curve of her belly as she swayed her hips sensuously. She glanced at Lynn with feigned surprise. "What is it?" she asked, and her eyes were wide and innocent.

"All right, Fay," said Lynn sullenly. "You can have your clothes."

"That's so nice of you, sister," purred Fay. "Maybe just to make sure, I'll wait here till you get them for me."

Lynn snorted. I thought she looked rather pretty at that moment. A blush was staining her cheeks and her neck. She hurried across to the bedroom, and Fay looked back at me with artful, inquisitive eyes.

"Quite a prude, isn't she?"

I tried to look cool and unimpressed. But I wasn't fooling myself. I knew I was het up. Casually, I got out my pack and selected a cigarette. "Maybe she doesn't like blackmail," I suggested.

"That's a hard word to use," said Fay. "Don't forget my angle. I'm virtually a prisoner here."

"Maybe she's got good reasons," I suggested.

Fay shot me a sharp glance and decided to change the subject. "Don't you like my body?" she said, and gazed down at herself with caressing eyes.

"You'll get by," I said shortly.

Starting at her neck, she ran her hands over her body in a gentle caressing movement. When her hands reached her hips she said, "You did this," and pointed to a faint yellow bruise.

My eyes flicked at it and then flicked away. Most of the time I'd been talking to Fay I'd tried looking any way except at her. It wasn't that she didn't bear looking at – she was just doing things to me!

Lynn said loudly from the bedroom door: "All right, Fay, I've put your clothes out for you. You can dress now."

Fay gave me a cheeky, impudent smile, rolled her briefs up around her waist again and sauntered across to the bedroom, deliberately swaying her hips. She gave me a roguish look over her shoulder as though to say: "*I bet that got you all steamed up, brother.*"

She was right too. And how!

Lynn closed the bedroom door on her and came across to me. "I'm terribly sorry about this."

"You don't have to worry. She hasn't killed me."

"You see the way it is, Hank. I'm worried about her. Sometimes she doesn't even seem to live in this world. I mean, what normal girl would behave like that?"

"Not many," I agreed. "But then, aren't you forgetting something?"

"Such as?"

"Fay got what she wanted," I pointed out. "Could she have got it any other way?"

Lynn stared at me with troubled eyes. "But a normal girl wouldn't go to those lengths," she said.

"That depends. If a dame wants something bad enough, she'll do almost anything to get it, sometimes."

Lynn's eyes were still worried. "Stick around, Hank," she pleaded. "I've got an uneasy feeling she might do *anything*."

"I'll stick," I said.

Fay came out of the bedroom. She was humming a tune and proudly self-conscious that she was dressed. She was wearing a black flared skirt and an off-the-shoulder Hungarian blouse. The blouse was purposely transparent so it could show the embroidery on the under-slip. Fay said, "How do I look, fella?" and twirled in front of me, the skirt flaring over her knees.

"You look swell," I said.

She crossed to the radio and switched it on. There was a dance band playing. "Come on," she said lightly. "Let's dance."

My eyes caught Lynn's. Lynn nodded imperceptibly and I got up and took Fay in my arms. Lynn went through to the kitchen and carried on with the cooking. Fay held my fingers tightly, thrust her belly hard against mine and, as we danced, laughed in my face challengingly.

"Look, Fay," I said. "I don't feel much like dancing."

"So you're yella," she challenged.

"All right," I said grimly. "If you want to dance ..." I went to work at dancing. I jitterbugged. I twirled her away from me like I wanted her to hit the wall, and jerked her back so hard that she bounced off my chest. At the end of two minutes, she was breathless, unable to keep up with my steps, and badly shaken. "I've had enough, Hank," she managed to gasp.

"That suits me fine," I said. I let her go when she was off balance, so she almost sprawled on the floor. I walked across to the radio, switched it off, went into the kitchen. Lynn was peeling potatoes. I picked up a knife and started on the potatoes alongside her.

The two girls had retired to their bedroom, leaving me with the settee, two pillows and a blanket. Lynn had pressed me to say so I could have an early-morning swim, and I hadn't resisted her invitation.

I took off my shoes and jacket, stretched myself on the settee, which was six inches too short, turned off the table lamp and tucked the blanket around me.

I musta drifted off to sleep fairly easily. The next thing I knew was awakening to a thumping sound and the muffled voice of a dame.

I sprang off the bed, switched on the table lamp and ran across to the bedroom. I opened the door and switched on the light. The room was empty, but the door of the bathroom was closed and locked. I could see the key in the lock, and Lynn was the other side, thumping with her fists and yelling for me.

And then, above the din that Lynn was making, I heard the sound of somebody trying to start a car engine. I didn't waste time on Lynn. I went out through the French windows and ran along the gravel path alongside the bungalow, barely noticing in my haste that I wasn't wearing shoes. A figure was sliding out of the driving seat of my hire-car.

I mentally congratulated myself for remembering the secret cut-out to the car and went after Fay, who was running hard.

I caught up with her and put my arms around her waist, dragging her to a stop. She twisted around and struck out at my face, savagely. She was breathing heavily and desperate to get away from me.

I grabbed her right hand with my left, bent low until my shoulder was against her thighs and wrapped my right arm around her legs. Then I jerked on my left hand, so that she sprawled across my shoulder, and at the same moment straightened myself up.

I was using what is known as the fireman's lift, and very effective it proved to be. All she could do was kick at the air savagely and beat at the small of my back with her free hand. She did both these things, but neither of them got me worried. I walked back to the bungalow slowly, knowing that the blood was running to her head and that she'd tire pretty soon. Half way back, she stopped struggling and pleaded with me to put her down. I didn't take any notice. Then she began to cry. I had seen how scheming this dame could be. I just let her keep on crying.

I went around the house again, back into the living room through the French windows, and through the bedroom to the bathroom door. Lynn was still battering on the door, but her voice was weaker now. I opened the door, and she almost fell out. "Thank heavens you've got her," she gasped as she saw the bundle I was carrying.

Fay gave a whimper. "Let me down," she pleaded.

"That's what happens when I let her have clothes," complained Lynn. "She waited until I went to the bathroom, locked me in, dressed herself and tried to skip."

"Better put a wrap on," I suggested gently.

Lynn was wearing a nightie. It was a black georgette nightie. Her flesh gleamed through it the same way it had gleamed through the fourth of the five veils. I didn't object, but my memories and emotions were being aroused, and this was no time to have my mind distracted.

Lynn blushed in that charming way of hers and struggled into a wrap.

I walked across to the big double bed the girls shared and humped Fay onto it. She hit it hard and the springs bounced her up again. The hem of her skirt slipped up to her lap as she swung her legs off the bed. I grabbed her hair and jerked her back.

"Better stay put, Fay," I warned.

She made a movement as though she was going to make another attempt to break for it. Then she caught my eye, and I must have looked as though I meant what I said. She sunk back, sitting there glaring at me sullenly.

"What do we do now?" asked Lynn wearily.

"You had the right idea the first time," I growled. "Better keep her clothes locked away."

Fay scowled. "I'm not taking my clothes off."

"You must be reasonable," pleaded Lynn.

"You can't keep me here," flared Fay. "I'm not going to be kept a prisoner."

Lynn looked at her solemnly and said: "Be sensible, Fay. If you won't stop with me ... you'll have to go back."

Fay tossed her head angrily. "Let *them* find me," she challenged.

Lynn looked at me questioningly. I shrugged my shoulders. "It's up to you," I said.

"Get undressed and let's go to bed," pleaded Lynn.

"I'm not undressing," said Fay determinedly.

I'd stayed in case Lynn hit up against trouble. Lynn *had* hit trouble. I was there to help her. And there was only one thing I could do. I moved in quickly, crooked my arm around Fay's neck, and held her arms behind her back.

"Get her skirt off," I said roughly.

"I don't like having to do this," began Lynn.

"Hurry up," I snapped.

Lynn manoeuvred around Fay's kicking legs, unzipped the skirt and worked it down around Fay's ankles.

"Leave it that way," I said. "It'll stop her kicking."

It was more difficult removing the blouse, because I had to release Fay's arms.

But we managed it somehow between us, and after that we stripped off Fay's hand-embroidered under-slip. It was history repeating itself. Fay was back again to her white briefs.

Fay was good and mad by this time, and I had to hold her while Lynn carefully locked the clothes away in the wardrobe, which fortunately had a strong lock. Then Lynn took her own clothes through to the living room and put them under my pillow. "I'll feel safer if you keep these till the morning," she said.

Fay realised then that she was beat. I let her go, and she sat there on the bed with her knees under her chin, her cheeks flushed with anger and her eyes misty with tears of exasperation.

"You gonna be all right here, Lynn?" I asked.

Lynn looked at Fay. "How about it, Fay?" she asked.

Fay looked at Lynn with angry eyes. Then she glanced at me. "You big cheese," she said contemptuously, and wriggled her legs down inside the bed-clothes and cushioned her cheek on the pillow.

"It's all right now, Hank," said Lynn. "I don't know how to thank you."

"Don't bother," I said. "Don't bother. Give me a yell if you want me again."

I went across to the door and stopped with my hand on the door-knob. "I won't close the door," I warned her. "Just in case."

I got back to the settee, and shortly afterwards heard the bed creak as Lynn climbed in beside Fay. It was a long while before I fell asleep.

The sun was shining through the windows when Lynn awakened me by shaking my shoulder. I sat up, stretched my aching limbs and yawned loudly. Lynn smiled. "Not so comfortable?" she asked.

"I feel like I gotta corrugated spine through sleeping in a ploughed field."

She laughed again. "I'll get some coffee for you. Can I have my clothes now?"

I got up and moved the pillow. "Help yourself," I said. "I hope they're not too creased."

Lynn bent down to pick them up, and the front of her wrap came open. I said: "Just a minute, Lynn."

She looked at me enquiringly.

"Stand up straight," I said.

Her eyes were wondering. But she stood up straight, facing me. I moved in close, slipped my hands in under the wrap and around her so I could strain her to me. I covered her mouth with mine, and she wasn't resisting. Two arms went around my neck and pulled tightly, while her body moulded into mine. Through the filmy nightgown I could feel the warmth of her body and a kinda nervous excited quivering.

"Hey, Lynn," yelled Fay from the bedroom. "Do I get my clothes this morning?"

Lynn pushed herself away from me, breathing heavily. "Here we go again," she said.

I jerked her to me again and gave her another rough and savage kiss. Savage because of the intensity of the emotion I was feeling, and because the warmth of her body was on my hands and the smell of her hair in my nostrils.

She broke it up. "Don't, Hank," she said. "We can't. Not here. Fay's calling again."

She snatched up her clothes and hurried back to the bedroom. I paced up and down for some moments, then went through to the kitchen and stuck my head under the tap. The cold water drumming down on the nerve centres at the back of my neck cooled me and made me feel more comfortable.

There wasn't much conversation at breakfast. Fay still hadn't got her clothes and she was scowling heavily. She sat at the table in her wrap and, as a sullen but hopeless gesture of defiance, didn't bother to tie the girdle. All she was wearing was the, by now very familiar, white briefs.

But she was cutting no ice. And she knew it. Both Lynn and I ignored her semi-nudity, and while we talked, Fay sat there watching us furtively, her face twisted into a disgruntled expression that at the same time contrived to be attractive.

Later, I saw Fay do some work for the first time. She washed up.

69

I took Lynn on one side and said: "Are you gonna be all right? I've got to go to town on business."

"I'll be all right, Hank," she said. "I've got her clothes locked away and I've hidden the wardrobe key. I've hidden the key of the car, too."

I patted her on the shoulder encouragingly. "It'll be all right soon," I reassured her. "You've got to give her time to settle down."

"I know," she said. "It's always a matter of time."

Fay grunted a grudging farewell when I left, and coupled it with a sullen stare.

Lynn came out front with me, and the last I saw of her was through the driving mirror. She looked cool and desirable in her blue and white check-print frock as she waved to me.

CHAPTER SEVEN

I made the rounds in town. Marshal Cleve Sanders had no further information for me. I checked up with him on Jake Peters' angle.

"No good, son," he said. "We've checked up on it, but it doesn't get us anywhere. But I'm still checking and I'll keep checking. Right to the last moment." His words sounded a little bitter. They struck an ominous note, too.

"The boy will get some extra time," I said.

He looked at me sharply, and his eyes twinkled approvingly.

"Are you behind this *habeas corpus* writ?"

"I dropped a word here and there."

"You're a straight guy," he said. "I guess I had you figured wrong when you first came." Then his face became worried again. "But if things stay the way they are, it ain't gonna help. The boy will have to come to trial sometime."

"Just keep checking," I encouraged.

"It'd be easier," he complained, "if only we had a photograph of Ellis Tundall."

I got an idea. "Check up with folks who know him," I said. "See if anybody who knew him has the ability to draw. We might get a likeness that way."

"It's an angle," said the Marshal. But he didn't sound very enthusiastic. "I'll try it. But I guess there ain't all that much artistic talent in the whole of Benton."

I went to see Jake Peters, who was door-keeping at the City Hall, but didn't get any further with him than I had before. Then I went out to Johnny Peters' garage and poked around for a coupla hours. The cops had been trampling all over there for hours. I didn't expect to find anything, and no miracles happened.

I returned to my hotel and telephoned the Chief. I told him there was no progress, and he sounded gloomy.

"Just stick to it, Hank," he said. "Just stick to it. We may get a break somewhere."

I wolfed down some lunch and then, because there was nothing else I could do that day, I drove back to Lynn's bungalow.

The first thing I noticed when I entered the drive was that the blue car was missing.

There was a strange tightness in my chest as I climbed out from the driving seat and ran around to the front of the house.

The French windows were wide open but the living room was deserted. I ran across to the bedroom and found it was locked.

"Lynn," I yelled. "Are you all right?"

She was in there right enough. She called out: "Hank, get me out, will you? Get me out."

Her voice sounded weak and pained, and I felt a sudden frightening anxiety for her. I retreated a coupla paces and hurled myself at the door. It was fragile and brittle, a typical bungalow construction. I nearly went clean through it. The lock snapped off and the door smashed back against the wall and hung at an angle, loose from one hinge.

But I wasn't worried about the door. It was Lynn I was thinking of. She was lying on the floor, stripped of all her clothes except a pair of flimsy cami-knickers. Her wrists were tied behind her back and her ankles drawn up so they could be secured to her wrists.

My heart was hammering madly as I picked her up and carried her across to the bed. There was an ugly red trickle seeping through her silky hair and dribbling down her cheek.

"Lynn," I gasped. "You all right, Lynn?"

I broke my nails untying the knots in the stocking that had been used to bind her. Lynn had been tied with savage force, and she must have been enduring agonies from restricted circulation.

As she tensed herself against the pain of the returning circulation, I examined her injury. She had a nasty lump, and the skin had been broken. I bathed the wound gently.

"Fay?" I asked.

She nodded miserably. "I didn't dream she'd do anything like this."

"What did it?"

She gave a little chuckle that broke off into a sob of pain as I dabbed at her scalp. "It sounds funny," she said. "A rolling pin. We were in the kitchen at the time."

"It could have been serious," I said.

She said, suddenly afraid: "Fay is here, isn't she?"

"The car's gone," I said briefly.

She sat up. For the first time, she realised she was wearing only a scanty under-garment. She said wildly: "She's gone, Hank. She's gone."

"What did you expect?" I said.

"Well, don't stay here," she said fiercely. "Get after her. Don't let her get away, Hank."

"I can't leave you, honey," I said. "You want looking after."

She became almost frantic. "Go after her, Hank," she ordered. "Every second counts. She can't be far away."

I looked at her, thought of how this was the first chance we'd had to be alone together, and then saw the appeal in her eyes.

"All right," I grunted. "I'll find her."

"Hurry," she said.

"What's she wearing?"

She dropped her eyes. "My clothes, I guess."

"How did she get the car keys?"

"They were in the pocket of my frock," she said.

I looked at her doubtfully. "I hate to leave you, honey," I said.

"Hank," she said earnestly, "if you ... like me ... go after her, will you? Don't waste any more time."

"O kay," I said quietly. "I'll find her."

I went out and climbed into my hire-car. I knew Fay hadn't driven into Benton, because I'd have passed her on the road. I took the other direction and pressed my foot down on to the accelerator. It sounded easy saying I'd find Fay, but I knew inside me that there was very little chance. Then I thought again. The first thing Fay would do, I reasoned, would be to ditch the car. She'd try for other transport. And I knew that this road went to Dalwood Junction. That was the nearest railway station to Benton. It was a hunch. But it was a hunch worth trying.

I really stepped on it then, and twenty minutes later I roared into Dalwood Junction and speeded through the high street up to the station approach. There were seven cars parked there, and my heart jumped as I recognised one of them.

I climbed out of the driving seat and ran across to the station. A thick-set, uniformed man spread himself across the entrance and said, as though it gave him great satisfaction: "Too late, bud. The train's just going."

I looked over his head at the short suburban train that was just beginning to move out.

"How long since a train left here?" I asked. "Going either direction."

"Coupla hours, bud. You've got two hours to wait before the next." He smacked his lips with satisfaction.

"That's the train I want," I said. I placed one hand in the centre of his chest and shoved hard. He was a short guy, but broad and stubby. There was plenty of substance there, and it surprised me the way he tottered back a coupla paces and fell on his hereafter.

I didn't waste time helping him up again. I sprinted across the platform, and sprinted alongside the train. It gathered speed and overtook me. I still kept on running. The last coach came level with me and slipped past. As I'd hoped, the coach was open at the back. It was moving fast as the open end drew level with me and I made a wild jump. My hands caught the passenger rail, and for a moment it felt like I was being strung out horizontal. And then my foot came down with a thud on the step that felt like my ankle was broken.

"Neatest bit of train catching I ever did see," said a fat-looking guy smoking a cigar and wearing a stetson. He gave me a hand and helped me up.

"Thanks," I said. I could hardly say it, I was breathing so hard.

"Reminds me of the time I almost missed the overnight express to Cactus," he said conversationally.

I looked back along the line. The station was out of sight now. I vaguely wondered if the ticket collector would wanna make trouble and telephone along the line.

"There was just ten minutes to go," the guy with the stetson was telling me. "I knew I could just make it, and then the taxi lost a wheel …"

I interrupted him brusquely. "Where's the next stop?"

He didn't like being interrupted. He stared at me, frowned, fished in his waistcoat pocket for a turnip-sized watch, which he consulted in terrifying earnestness, then said: "I calculate we'll be in Morton in thirty-three and one half minutes."

I nodded my thanks and started to open the door leading into the train corridor. The ticket collector was working his way down along the corridor, looking in at each of the compartments.

I ducked back and said to the fat guy: "Have you got a ticket?"

"Sure," he said. "They're awful tough on fellas who try travelling light."

"I haven't got a ticket," I said simply.

"I'll bet you were in too awful a hurry to get one, eh?" He chuckled deep down in his throat, and his fat little belly wobbled.

I had a mental picture of the ticket inspector at Dalwood Junction breathing fire and brimstone into the telephone. I had a mental picture of myself being escorted from the train to the cop station while Fay disappeared into nowhere.

"You're a college man?" I asked.

"Durwent man," he said proudly. "My sons are there now."

"I'm a Durwent man," I said.

"Well, are you now?" he said enthusiastically. He held out his hand and shook mine vigorously. "Shoulda guessed it," he said. "It'd take a Durwent man who's good at ball games to get on a train the way you did. What year were you there?"

"Look," I said. "I'm in a spot. I knocked over the ticket collector to get on this train. Back me up, will you?"

That was all I had time to say. The ticket inspector opened the door and came out on to the platform. "Tickets, please," he said. He eyed me curiously. Maybe he was wondering how I got there. The man with the stetson looked at me doubtfully. He fumbled in his pocket and produced a ticket. I looked at him appealingly and he fumbled some more. "That's funny," he mused. "I had them both a minute ago."

The ticket collector and I stood and stared at the man with the stetson as, slowly and methodically, he turned out every one of his pockets. When he had turned out the last one, he looked at the ticket inspector despairingly. He shrugged his shoulders with palms held outwards.

The inspector said seriously: "Can't ride without a ticket."

"Don't worry, John," I said to the man with the stetson. "I guess we can find the price of a ticket." I pulled out my wallet.

"Where did you get on?" asked the ticket inspector.

"Moose Point," said the man with the stetson quickly.

"That'll be two-forty-five," said the inspector.

I handed over the notes and pocketed my change.

"Well," breathed the stetsoned man, when the inspector had gone. "We Durwent men must stick together."

"I sure am grateful," I said.

"Skip it," he said. "Have a cigar. What year did you say you were there?"

All this had taken quite a time, and the train was slowing down now. "This must be Morton," I said.

He consulted his watch again. "That's right," he agreed. "Dead on time." He sounded happy. "What year did you say?"

The train ground to a stop and I hung out over the platform and watched the descending passengers. My heart leapt as I saw a familiar blue and white check-print frock making towards the exit.

"Eighteen eighty-eight," I yelled at the man in the stetson, and jumped down on to the platform. I tried elbowing my way through the crowd, but only earned myself a lot of nasty looks. I was simmering inside, but had to wait my turn.

When I got outside, I looked up and down. There was no blue and white check frock in sight. But the station bus was standing nearby and, as I looked, it began to move off. Through the windows I caught a glimpse of Fay about to settle down in one of the seats.

I ran across the road to a taxi rank. "Follow that bus," I yelled at the driver.

He nodded and got out to open the door for me. "Hurry," I said.

He nodded and went round the front and began to crank the engine. The fourth time he cranked, it still didn't start. I was out of the cab and standing beside him, almost pleading with him. "Put a move on, will you?" I said.

He took his cigarette from his mouth, spat deliberately on the ground and said: "No hurry, mister. First bus stop is twenty miles away. I can catch that bus before then." He fixed me with a penetrating eye. "It's a long drive. It'll cost you a lotta dough."

I pulled out my wallet and flashed a roll of notes at him. "Catch that bus," I said. "There's ten extra for you."

That made a difference. The engine fired first time. He was in the driver's seat before I was inside the cab. He started off while the door was still open. Ten minutes later, the bus was in sight.

"Just keep tailing her," I said. "I'm keeping check on a dame wearing a blue and white frock."

He looked over his shoulder at me and grinned impudently. "Wife trouble, huh?"

"Just keep the bus in sight," I growled.

The bus stopped at a small town called Windend. And that's where Fay got off. And by this time, I'd had a chance to do some figuring. It seemed to me that Fay was acting like she was going to some place. It didn't seem to me like she was just running out. She had somewhere fixed in mind.

My hunch was right. When she got off the bus, the taxi driver tailed her at a walking pace. She knew exactly where she was going. She turned left off the main drag, and half-way down the block walked straight into a hotel. The driver pulled up outside. "Going any further?" he asked.

"That's the end of the line," I said.

"Take my advice," he said. "Ditch her first chance you get and don't make the mistake of getting married a second time."

"You wanna watch sometime you don't tread on your nose," I warned him.

Immediately I saw the reception clerk I knew he was my man. There was a slick, crafty air of efficiency about him that typified him.

I walked across to the reception desk and, without saying a word, slowly took out my wallet, flashed out a ten dollar bill and put it on the desk in front of him.

He looked at the bill, looked at me, looked back at the bill, picked it up and stowed it away in his pocket. "He is as good as dead," he said.

This reception clerk had been to the movies. He knew he should ask: "*Who do I have to kill?*" He'd gone one better.

I said shortly: "A dame in a blue and white check frock just came in."

"Mrs Robinson. Room 37, second floor," he said. "Want me to announce you?" He grinned impudently.

"I'll find my own way up."

I was half-way to the stairs when he called: "Hey, mister, just a minute."

I went back. He said: "Maybe you'd like to know. Mr Robinson will be back any minute."

"Mr Robinson?" I said. I musta looked surprised.

"Yeah! Didn't you know?"

I thought that over quickly. "Was Mr Robinson expecting Mrs Robinson?"

"He's been here a week," said the clerk. "Been expecting her any time, I guess. Left word I was to give her the key so she could go straight up if he was out."

I nodded at him shortly. "Thanks a lot."

I hesitated outside the door, wondering if I should knock. I decided against it and pushed right on in. Fay was sitting at the dressing table, combing her hair. She jumped to her feet and stared in astonishment.

"Good afternoon, Mrs Robinson," I said, and I hung my hat on the rack just inside the door.

"You!" she said incredulously. "How did you get here?"

I looked around the room, tested the bed, noticed the three big leather suitcases on the suitcase stand and sauntered over to them.

"How did you get here?" she repeated.

"Inspiration, honey," I said. "I just felt like coming into this hotel."

She said imperiously: "Get out. Get out before I complain to the manager."

"I wouldn't do that, honey," I said, casually. "You wouldn't want to go back to St Louis, would you?"

Her eyes filled with sudden apprehension, and her tone changed. "Why don't you leave me alone, fella?" she said. "Why don't you let me live my own life?"

Experimentally, I pulled the catch on one of the suitcases. It snapped open. I pulled up the lid and looked inside. At a quick glance I could see there were men's clothes there, and what looked like a collection of safe deposit keys.

"How dare you," screamed Fay. She was across the room and around in front of me slamming the lid almost as soon as I'd got it open. "You're going too far," she said.

I chuckled and lit myself a cigarette as I sat on the bed, swinging my legs. "And how's Mr Robinson?" I asked.

Her lips twisted sullenly. "Why don't you get out of my life?" she demanded.

I looked at the ceiling and said casually: "Lynn is in hospital. Seems like she's got a bad case of fracture." I dropped my eyes and watched Fay beneath my eyelids.

For a moment I saw a gleam of horror in her eyes, which was immediately replaced by sullen defiance. "That's her fault," she retorted. "She shouldn't have interfered with me."

I looked at her through narrowed lids. "What's driving you, baby?" I asked. "What makes you so anxious to see this fella Robinson that you'd even injure your own sister?"

She tried to stare me out, and then her eyes dropped. "He's a friend of mine," she said quietly. "I knew him before I was married. He was in touch with me while I was in .." Her voice broke off, but I knew she meant the asylum.

"So now you're having a grand reunion and will live happy ever after," I said sarcastically.

"Hank, be a good fella," she pleaded. "Just leave me alone, will you?"

"Sure," I said. "I'll leave you to it. When I've seen Mr Robinson."

She sighed with exasperation. For a moment she looked like she was going to blow her top. Then she paced over to the window. She stood there nervously tugging her handkerchief. I leaned back against the head of the bed and watched her, drooling smoke through my nostrils.

A little later there was the sound of footsteps in the corridor. Fay turned and faced the door, her body tensed with excitement. I got up too.

The door opened wide, and in came Robinson. Fay ran across the room and threw herself into his arms, sobbing with joy, clinging to him like she was afraid she'd never see him again.

His face scowled at me over her shoulder, and I scowled back.

"What are you doing here, Janson?" he demanded.

"How were things in jail, Mr Edward Trice?" I said, spitting the words out contemptuously.

"Get away from me, Fay," said Trice ominously.

She clung to him. "It's so good to see you, Eddie," she sobbed. "I love you, darling. I won't ever leave you again."

"Get away from me," he said.

"My darling, my darling," she moaned, still clinging to him.

He put his hand against her chest and shoved hard so that she hurtled backwards. Her legs hit against a chair, and she hit the carpet. Trice didn't even give her a second glance. "Get out of here, Janson," he said.

Eddie Trice hadn't altered much in the five years that had elapsed since he had been arrested for his bestial treatment of his wife. I guess I hadn't altered much either, since he'd recognised me straight away.

"Fay got a divorce from you," I said.

"She's altered her mind about that. She's back with me now."

"You've got it added up wrong," I told him. "Fay's loose on condition she's in the care of her sister. You don't happen to be her sister, do you?"

"Fay and me are getting married right away," he said. "You don't think you can get her away from me now, do you?"

Fay had climbed to her feet and was listening to this conversation with amazement on her face. She burst in quickly: "Do you know him, Eddie?"

Eddie gave a sour grin. "He's the fella who gave me all that unpleasant publicity just before the trial."

She stared at me apprehensively, and her hand went up to her mouth nervously. "I didn't know that, Eddie," she said.

"Fay's coming back with me," I told him.

He shook his head slowly, grinning mirthlessly. "You can't do that, fella," he said. "She's a right to remain free as long as she can. She can't be taken back by anybody except legal officers. And they'll have to get a warrant first." He smoothed his wispy moustache, and I noticed the dirty bandage around his wrist.

"I can get a warrant," I said. "If Fay won't go with me now, what say I telephone the Marshal of Benton. He'll get a warrant."

He shook his head again and grinned even more sourly. "You oughta read up the law, fella," he said. "Cleve Sanders hasn't any authority to issue those kinda warrants."

"Maybe I'll have a word with him, just the same," I said.

"Yeah, but do it somewhere else, will you?" he said in a bored tone. "I'm paying for the rent of this room."

Fay said quickly: "Get rid of him, Eddie. I've had trouble enough getting away from Lynn. He must have followed me."

Trice jerked his thumb over his shoulder. "Scram, hawkeye," he said. "Get going. Hit the road. Scram!"

I stood there for a moment, wondering what I should do. Legally he was in the right. To all intents and purposes, right at this moment, Fay was a free woman. I had no right to start putting the arm on her.

"Okay, Trice," I said. "I guess I'd better go back to Benton and go into it. But I'm warning you, if Fay finds herself in trouble, I'll put the finger on you."

"Scram," he said. "Hit the dust. Blow, willya?"

I walked thoughtfully down the stairs, and when I got to the reception desk I booked a room for myself. "Is there a garage near here?" I asked.

"Right across the road."

"How about that guy Robinson? Has he got a car?"

"In the car park," he said. "Entrance is just at the side. Registration number three-two-two-zero-zero."

I nodded. "Ten dollars earns a little silence as well," I told him.

He grinned. "That's okay, mister. I always keep my lip buttoned."

I walked across the road to the garage and slipped a quick look up at the windows of Trice's room. I saw the curtains move slightly and knew that he was watching me.

There were three guys working on an old wreck. I said to one: "There's more profitable things you can be doing."

"Such as what?"

"Taking a ride in a hire-car."

"Whose car?"

"Yours," I said.

"Okay, buddy," he said. "Draw a picture. What are you getting at?"

"The hotel opposite," I told him. "Shortly after I'm gone, a car number three-two-two-zero-zero is gonna come out of the car park. I wanna know where that car heads. I wanna know where it stops. Do I make myself clear?"

"Are you a shamus?" he asked.

I dived down in my pocket and produced one of my cards.

"The *Chronicle* pays full expenses," I told him, and then added, "and tips."

He looked satisfied. "Okay, bud. I'll do it." He rubbed his forefinger and thumb together meaningfully. "How about a little something to show good faith?"

I passed him twenty bucks and said: "When I'm gone, if anybody asks any questions, tell them I was enquiring for a hire-car, which you couldn't supply."

"There's a bus going to Benton in ten minutes," he told me.

"That's fine," I told him. "I'll catch the bus. And when you get the information I want, I'll be in the hotel across the way. You've got the name on the card."

I walked slowly to the bus stop and took care not to look over my shoulder. When the bus came, I surged forward with the other passengers and climbed inside. I shot a quick look through the window and caught a glimpse of somebody standing on the far corner, shielding his eyes as though trying to see inside the bus. The bus started, and the man standing on the corner stood watching until the bus was well under way. Then he turned around and disappeared back along the side street where the hotel was. I hadn't much doubt that it was Trice.

I got off at the next stop, crossed the road and caught the next bus back. As soon as I got into the hotel, the reception clerk said: "You sure scared them birds, brother. They breezed out right after you."

"I'll keep my room, just the same," I told him. "And there's a fella from the garage will be calling in later."

"What do you want I should do with him?"

"Send him up."

To pass the time, I took a shower. After that I rang for a whisky and soda, and shortly afterwards the garage hand arrived and reported that he had successfully followed Trice and Fay.

Eddie Trice had been sharp. He'd checked at the garage, asked what I wanted, made sure I'd got the bus for Benton and then lit out immediately. He'd holed up in a little cabin ten miles out of town and, coincidentally, it was on the river Mississippi. From the garage mechanic's description, it seemed a poor kinda place to hole out in.

I got Lynn on the phone after that. I assured her that Fay was all right. I gently broke to her the news that Fay had been communicating with Eddie for some time, and that she was now back with him.

"But this is terrible, Hank," she said.

"Don't worry, honey," I said. "I've got it all in hand. I know where they are, and I'll keep a check on them." I gave Lynn the address and told her to come on over the following day and meet me there.

"I'll come right away," she said.

"Lynn," I said seriously. "You've asked me to help you. I'm doing the best I can. Do what I ask, willya, kid? Come on over tomorrow. I'll handle this tonight. There's special angles."

"I don't like it, Hank."

"Don't you trust me?" I asked.

There was silence for a moment. "Of course I do, Hank."

81

"Trust me a bit more, honey," I said. "Come over tomorrow. Get there about twelve."

"All right, Hank," she said quietly. "I'll do what you want."

After that, I put through a call to Cleve Sanders, Marshal of Benton.

"Hank Janson speaking," I told him.

"Still nothing developed."

"Look," I said, "you told me that if I ever needed your help, I'd get it. Does that still go?"

"Sure," he said. "That goes."

"I'm playing a hunch," I said. "I need your help. Will you come on over here tomorrow? Arrive about ten and wait for me to telephone." I gave him the address of my hotel.

"I wanna help, Janson," he said. "But I ain't used to wearing blinkers."

"Maybe I'm doing this all wrong," I said. "But I want you to string along. I'd like to tell you more, but I can't right now because it's such a wild guess I'm making that you'd be scared out of your pants."

"Nothing scares me, son," he said.

"But you're legal-minded," I told him. "Maybe there's something it's better you didn't know."

He still sounded doubtful. "I don't think I ought to do this, son," he said.

"I've got nobody else to rely on."

"Okay," he yielded. "I don't like it, but I'll do it. I'll be over there tomorrow at ten."

"There's just one other thing," I said. "Bring Jake Peters with you."

"Bring Jake Peters!" he echoed.

"Yeah, give him a day off from door-keeping. He'll enjoy himself looking at all the folks he sees on the way over."

"It seems a crazy way of doing things to me," grumbled Cleve.

"It may be crazy," I agreed. "But if there's any fumbling, there's only gonna be one guy takes the rap, and that's me."

I hung up on that note. I went over everything in my mind again, adding up all those little things that don't seem to amount to anything until you fit them in the right places, and although there were plenty of empty spaces that I filled in with my imagination, the completed jigsaw seemed to have coherence.

I finished off my whisky and then climbed into my jacket. I was off to keep Fay and Trice company during the long night hours.

CHAPTER EIGHT

I got the garage mechanic to drive me out to where he had followed Eddie and Fay.

It was ten miles outta town, well off the highway and in a secluded position. The mechanic stopped the car and pointed to two dimly-lit windows a hundred yards down the road. "That's the place," he said.

"That'll be fine," I told him. "I'll walk the rest."

It was a tourist's cabin, intended for fishermen who didn't mind roughing it. When I got right up close, I could see it was made of Canadian timber. There wasn't even a garage. Eddie's car was parked on the grass verge just off the road.

I tried looking in through the windows first. That didn't get me anywhere. The curtains had been carefully drawn. Then I went around the cabin to the river side and knocked at the only door the cabin boasted.

There were movements from inside, a kinda surprised hesitancy. One of the curtains moved slightly, and I slid into the shadows by the door. After a reasonable pause, I knocked again. There were more movements inside, and then the door opened about two inches, just enough for Fay to peep through. "Who is it?" she asked cautiously.

I didn't give her time even to finish the sentence. I had my shoulder against the door and I thrust hard. The door opened wide, sweeping Fay along with it as though she was being swept along by a broom.

I stepped inside with my hands in my pockets, looked around the room – barely glancing at Eddie, who had climbed to his feet with a look of surprise on his face – and said cheerily: "Evening, folks."

A kinda stunned silence greeted me. Eddie had been seated at the table in his shirtsleeves. He had stood up so quickly that he'd upset his chair. For a moment, the tension was so thick you could have taken it and cut it in slices. Eddie flashed a look at Fay, who was staring at him in silence. "Shut the door," he said.

Fay shut the door and stood with her back against it. Eddie was breathing hard, and his arms hung at his sides so that his clenched fists rested on the table top. "What do you want?" he demanded, and his voice was filled with menace.

I assumed an unconcerned expression and glanced around the cabin. It was a single room affair, roughly furnished and with a bunk on either side of the room. A little doorless annexe led to a tiny kitchen. I removed my fedora and skimmed it across the room towards the dresser. I was lucky this time. It made a three-point landing. "Snug little place you've got here," I said casually.

"What do you want?" demanded Eddie again.

"Just a little chat."

Eddie flashed me an up-and-under look from his hooded eyes, bent down to retrieve his fallen chair and grunted to Fay. "Give him a chair, willya?"

Fay brought me a chair, and I sat opposite Eddie. He was watching me steadily, and I was waiting for any quick move he might make. But he kept both his hands on the table where I could see them.

"All right," he said, "what do you want?"

"It's about Fay."

His lip curled in a sneer. "Fay's my responsibility," he said. He glanced at Fay and jerked his thumb towards the kitchen. "Coffee," he said briefly.

Fay hurried across to the kitchen, and I turned and watched her. Most girls of spirit would have resented being ordered about that way. I knew Fay had plenty of spirit. It surprised me, the way she took it.

I looked back at him, and his eyes were grinning at me. "Useful dame to have around," he said.

"What makes you think she'll stick around?"

"She'll stick," he asserted confidently. "I've got what it takes."

"And just what does it take?" I asked him.

He chuckled. "You know how dames are. They'll do anything for the guy they love."

I glanced back at Fay. She must have heard every word Eddie said. But there was only placid acceptance on her face.

"Okay," I agreed. "So you've got the dame twisted around your little finger. But that ain't everything, Trice."

"We're reasonable men, I hope, Janson," he said. "Just what is it you want? If we talk this over, maybe we'll get somewhere."

I looked at him suspiciously. "There's only one thing I want. I want Fay to go back to her sister."

He shrugged his shoulders and spread his hands expressively. "Can I make her go back?" he asked.

"I don't see why not."

84

He looked at me thoughtfully, and then his face slowly creased in a grin. "What say we try it out, Janson? Fay," he yelled loudly. "Come here. Come right over here."

She came and stood beside him. "You heard what we've been saying," he said quietly.

"Yes, Eddie," she said meekly.

"All right. You'll go back with Janson," he said. "Understand?"

"I won't go," she said quietly but stubbornly.

"You won't go, eh?" His face creased in a scowl. "Kneel down, Fay," he said ominously.

Fay knelt down beside him, and Eddie twisted in his chair so that he was facing her. "I'm gonna give you one last chance," he said. "Are you gonna go away with Mr Janson?"

She dropped her eyes, somehow looking like a guilty heretic before the Inquisition. "No, Eddie," she said. "I won't leave you."

Eddie moved so quickly that it was all over before I could do anything. His fist flashed, there was the meaty sound of knuckles smacking against flesh, and Fay sprawled over backwards on the floor. I went hot all over, and half rose from my chair.

"Hold it," rapped Eddie. But he was only half watching me. He was watching Fay, who was scrambling to her knees in front of him and reaching out for the hand that had struck her. There were unshed tears of pain in her eyes and an ugly red abrasion beneath her eye, but she rested her cheek against his rough hand and closed her eyes as though overwhelmed with happiness. "I'll never leave you, Eddie," she said. "I love you."

Eddie jerked his hand away from her and said grimly: "I'll give you one more chance."

I said evenly: "If you hit that dame again, Eddie, I'll kill you."

"Don't be a dope," he said. "She can take it. She likes taking it."

"I've warned you," I said.

"Don't be a dope," he repeated. "Let the dame decide." Then he looked at Fay and said: "Are you gonna go with Janson?"

"I won't leave you, Eddie," she said, and her arms were hanging limply at her sides, and she almost seemed to lift her face expectantly towards Eddie's heavy, driving fist.

Fay went over backwards again, and her head hit the ground just about the same time that I got to my feet and swung across the table at Eddie. He'd been expecting that. He was off his chair and away from the table so that my swinging fist cut empty air.

I growled with rage, and made a swift encirclement of the table. Eddie did the same. There was a slightly scared look in his eyes as he yelled: "Don't be a dope, Janson. Let the dame decide."

I circled around the table again, and Eddie circled with me. He seemed remarkably light on his feet. "Let the dame decide, Janson," he yelled again, slightly desperate now.

"I'm going to teach you ..." I began.

At first impact, it felt like a small shell had hit me. It smashed against my side so hard that it jolted me clean off my feet onto my hereafter. I hit the ground with a heavy, painful thump. And at the moment I hit the ground, I realised it was Fay who had flung herself at me, head first. She was fighting mad. So surprised was I by the suddenness of the attack that I offered little resistance. Her weight thrust me back until my shoulders were touching the ground, and then she sat on my chest while she alternately tugged at my hair and slapped my face.

"Stop it," said Eddie commandingly. "Cut it out, Fay."

She stopped. I don't think I've ever seen any other dame whose individuality has been so completely dominated by a man. She sat there astride my chest, her skirts rucked up, showing her thighs almost to the hip. She was breathing heavily, and her long hair hung half over her face. But the hair didn't conceal her bruised, torn cheek.

"Let him get up," said Eddie.

Obediently she climbed to her feet and stood staring down at me with hateful, venomous eyes. I climbed to my feet slowly and eyed Eddie grimly. He was keeping the table between us. "I oughta punch your nose," I said.

"Don't be a dope, Janson," he said. "Start anything and the dame will be right in the middle of it. Anyway, I was only doing what you wanted. I told her to go with you. I've even beaten her. She still won't go. What do we do now?"

I looked at Fay. "Maybe you oughta do something about that cheek of yours," I said.

She smiled at me contemptuously. But already the redness was spreading around her eye, and a hint of blue was threatening the birth of a black eye.

"Nuts," growled Eddie. "That don't bother her any. Get the coffee."

With another sidelong glare at me, Fay went back to the kitchen and took up the coffee percolator.

"What say we sit and talk it over some more," said Eddie, and there was a slimy, confident grin on his face.

I looked at Fay, looked at him, sighed and pulled my chair up to the table again.

"It's up to you now," he said. "I've done my best. What do you suggest?"

"Her sister Lynn and I will take her away," I said.

"That's okay by me," he said genially. "Why don't you go get her?"

"That's what I intended to do this afternoon," I said. "Remember?"

"Oh, that," he said. He made a brushing movement with his hands. "We didn't like that hotel," he said with an impudent grin. "We decided we'd like it better here. Much more cosy."

"You forgot to leave a forwarding address."

"Did I now?" he said sarcastically. "Now wasn't that thoughtless of me?"

"Being that you're such a thoughtless kinda guy," I said, "maybe I'll stick around for a while."

"You're getting this all wrong, Janson," he said. "Since your visit this afternoon, I've been thinking things over. Maybe I ain't got no right to have Fay with me. I'm agreeable to anything you say. Tomorrow I'll take her back to Lynn myself. There. How does that suit you?"

"That suits me fine," I said, eyeing him narrowly. "If that's what you intend to do."

"Sure, Janson," he said. "I'll do just that."

"Just the same," I said, tilting my chair back onto the back legs, "I'll stick around."

"Stick as long as you like, fella," he said carelessly. His ready acquiescence startled me.

"I'll stick right here overnight until we get going in the morning," I said.

"That's okay," he agreed. "Sounds reasonable enough."

Fay put three cups and saucers on the table, poured hot milk and then coffee. Plenty of sugar went into the coffee, and she gave Eddie a cup, placed a cup in front of me and pulled a chair up to the table for herself.

I looked at Eddie wonderingly. There was a catch here somewhere, although I couldn't figure what it was. I looked at Fay. Her eyes were downcast, her attitude submissive. She seemed almost like the meek and submissive slave of the harem.

Eddie sipped his coffee. "Not bad," he said approvingly. Fay sipped her coffee. When she removed her lips from the cup, it was smeared with lipstick.

"That's good enough for me, Eddie," I said. "What say we change cups now?"

He looked at me with wide eyes, not understanding. Then, as I exchanged our cups, he understood what I was getting at. He chuckled loudly. "You've been reading too many detective stories,

87

Janson," he jeered. "Or else you've been reading the *Chicago Chronicle*. It's a real scandal rag," he added smoothly.

I eyed him steadily. "Nevertheless," I said, "what say you drink the coffee?"

He looked down at the cup and chuckled. "My, what an imagination you've got," he said.

"Drink the coffee," I said grimly.

"All in good time," he said. He produced a pack of cigarettes and we lit up. I sat there eyeing him across the table, and he was grinning at me; grinning at some joke I didn't appreciate. He still wasn't drinking his coffee. It was a waiting game. I sat there watching him, sipping my own coffee. And then, when I was almost through, Eddie said: "I like my coffee cold, you know, Janson," and then took his cup and drank slowly.

As he was drinking, his eyes were laughing at me. I suddenly felt very silly and very childish.

"Get the cards," ordered Eddie.

Fay came back with a pack of cards she had taken from Eddie's suitcase. He shuffled them, looking at me mockingly. "Since you're gonna be our guest tonight," he said, "we've gotta pass the time some way. What's your strength at poker?"

"My game's as good as my cards."

"I mean, what d'ya want to bet?"

"I play for bucks, not centuries."

"All right then. A little friendly game for bucks."

He dealt the cards, and Fay cleared the coffee cups away. Then Fay went across to one of the bunks, stretched herself out and began reading a magazine.

The game went on interminably. The air grew thick with smoke, and the hands of the clock crawled round past midnight. We still went on playing. I'd noticed a long while ago that he no longer had the bandage around his wrist. When he spread his cards out on the table, a triumphant grin on his face as he exhibited his full house, I saw the scar on his wrist. It was a scabby scar about one-and-a-half inches long, stretching in a straight line across his pulse. I said: "Looks like you've got yourself a cut there."

He glanced at it. "Yeah," he agreed. "Nasty cut it was."

"Strange place to get a cut," I said.

"Did it carving a joint," he explained. "Knife slipped."

"What's your job?" I asked. "Chef?"

He glared at me. "Your deal."

Fay was bored. She dropped her magazine and wandered over to the table. She stood behind Eddie and watched his cards.

88

She stood there for three or four hands, watching him with boredom and occasionally placing her hand over her mouth to suppress a yawn.

After that, she sauntered around to my side and looked over my shoulder. Eddie shot a sharp glance at her, but after that concentrated on his cards.

"Maybe Fay ought to get some sleep," I suggested.

"She can bed down if she likes."

Fay said tonelessly: "I'm not tired." I glanced over my shoulder at her, and she was just suppressing another yawn. I grinned. I guessed pretty soon she'd decide to lie down and get some shut-eye.

Eddie started to deal again. Fay moved away from behind me, and I glanced over my shoulder at her. She'd opened one of the curtains and was staring out into the night. I turned back to my cards and found I'd picked up a flush.

Eddie said he was staying. He raised. I raised him. He grinned confidently and raised again. I looked at my cards to confirm I had the flush, and raised him once more.

He said artfully: "I wonder which of us two is bluffing, if either of us?"

"Try me?" I suggested. "Raise me again."

He raised me again.

I put my cards on the table and started counting out the dough to raise him when the roof fell on my head. I wasn't knocked out cold. My skull felt like it had been shattered in a thousand pieces. But I was conscious enough to realise that Fay had smashed the vase on my head. It felt like bits of china mingled in with the fragments of my head, and water mingled with my blood. I knew I was slowly toppling sideways and tried to save myself. But my arms and legs were leaden, and when the floor hit my face, it seemed to be tilted at an angle of forty-five degrees.

Everything around me was blurred. I realised somehow I must get on my feet. I eased myself on to my hands, and through a thick fog saw Eddie's face leering at me. From a long way away, I saw his fist travelling towards me with the speed of a tortoise. It seemed to be travelling towards me for hours, getting bigger and bigger so that I could see the thick hairs on his fingers and his heavy gold ring. And then the fist exploded into sparks, and once again the floor was rubbing against my cheeks. I was struggling in a vast sea of mud that sucked at my limbs, tearing at them, twisting and hurting them. There were weights pressing on my chest and crushing my body. There was a loud roar in my ears, and the grey floor kept threatening to turn black.

I never completely passed out. I fought off the grey mist, and my shattered nerve cells slowly collected themselves together. I felt like I was lying on the floor with a riveter driving red-hot rivets into my brain. I gritted my teeth and tried to move, then discovered that my hands were bound behind my back. There were cords around my ankles, too.

That acted rather as a cold water sluice. It brought me back to consciousness far more quickly that anything else could have done. I glared up at Eddie and said: "Smart guy, eh?"

"That's right, Janson," he said. "I'm a smart guy."

He wasn't strong enough to lift me onto the bunk himself. He had to get Fay to help him.

I said grimly: "You aren't gonna get away with this. You're overplaying your hand."

"Think so?" he mused. "Well, we'll see, Janson."

I said to Fay: "Don't fall for this game, Fay. He's poison. Remember what he did to you before?"

"Shut up," said Eddie.

"Remember, Fay?" I said. I was trying to drive it into her that she'd be in for more trouble. "Remember, Fay? Think back to what happened?"

"Shut up," said Eddie again.

"You've got to listen to me, Fay," I pleaded. "This guy's not human. He'll crucify you."

Eddie went away and came back with a roll of sticking plaster. I tried to jerk my head away from him, but he got Fay to hold my head still while he stretched the plaster across my face, sealing my lips and successfully gagging me. I didn't feel very comfortable after that. I'm a guy that breathes in through my nose and exhales through my mouth. Making my nose do double the work it did normally got me feeling half-suffocated. I started sweating all over, my temperature soared and I felt I was gonna choke any minute.

Eddie sat down heavily and got his breath back. "Nice work, Fay," he said.

She went over to him and climbed onto his lap. He put his arms around her waist and she wrapped her arms around his neck. "I love you so much, Eddie," she almost moaned.

He unbuttoned the front of her dress, pulled the dress away to expose her white shoulder, and his thick fingers buried themselves in her soft flesh. His black eyes glittered at me mockingly as he gripped her savagely.

90

She moaned with pain, and clung to him more tightly. His brutal fingers gouged and bruised her. Fay continued moaning and clinging to him tightly. At last he pushed her from him roughly and said: "Get a drink."

She got up and went out to the kitchen. She came back with two glasses and a bottle of rye. Her dress still hung over her shoulder, and I could see the ugly red blotches his fingers had made on her skin. They were big glasses, tooth-brush size. Eddie poured himself three fingers, poured the same for Fay, and then his eyes gleamed. He chuckled. He started pouring into Fay's glass again. He went on pouring until the glass was full. The bottle was half empty.

"Drink, Fay," he said.

She looked at him and looked at the glass doubtfully. "I don't drink whisky, Eddie," she said.

His brow clouded. "Drink it," he said, with an angry note in his voice.

Fay gulped at the raw spirit. She musta been trying to get it over quickly. But the raw liquor was strong. It burnt her throat and took her breath. Tears spurted from her eyes, and she coughed like she'd never stop. Eddie sat there watching her with a sly grin on his face. When she had recovered from coughing, he pointed at her glass again. "Finish it," he said.

He made her gulp it down like it was lemonade. In five minutes she'd drunk as much Scotch as two guys together would drink in five hours. When she put the empty glass on the table, her eyes still spurted with tears and her voice was hoarse. She said: "I drank it, Eddie."

He looked at her curiously, climbed to his feet and stood in front of her. She stood facing him submissively, her hands drooping listlessly at her sides.

His greedy eyes looked her up and down slowly, and then his rough hands reached out, dragged her half-open dress down over her shoulders, pulling it down until it pinioned her arms at her side, and revealed starkly the white, soft flesh of her body. She stood there in front of him, meek, docile.

Eddie looked at her and chuckled. Then he flicked his eyes to me and smiled mockingly. "Kinda cute, ain't she, Janson?" he said.

I couldn't say anything with my mouth, but I said it all with my eyes. That made him chuckle some more.

"She's a queer dame, Janson," he said. "I treat her rough, and she likes it. Don't you, honey?" he said, turning to Fay.

91

She nodded her head slowly, looking at him appealingly. Her white shoulders and breasts were brazenly exposed to his contemptuous eyes. He reached out and twisted her around roughly, his thick fingers devoid of the tenderness her body craved. He thrust her in the direction of the other bunk, and she stumbled a few paces, almost falling. "Get over there," he growled. Then he turned to me, his face creased in a wicked grin. He winked broadly and said: "Sleep well, Janson."

He clicked off the electric light, and through the darkness I heard him shuffling across the room towards Fay and the bunk in the far corner. Shortly afterwards I heard him grunt with exertion, and Fay uttered a low, gurgling sob of pain. Eddie chuckled. Fay moaned again.

It went on like that for quite a while. Through the darkness, the sound of their movements became a graphic nightmare. Long after Eddie began to snore, Fay was still giving little whimpers of pain.

I wasn't too happy myself. The cords around my wrists felt like they were cutting right through the flesh. And I was having to watch my breathing. When I tried to breathe naturally, I got that choked, suffocating sensation. It was a wonder that under those circumstances I ever fell asleep.

I was awakened in the morning by the soft sound of Fay slipping out of bed. I watched her as she quickly climbed into her frock. She glanced at me and saw that my eyes were open and watching, but she glanced away again as though I was of no account. Then she pulled back the curtains, and the bright sunlight streaming in through the windows fell across Eddie's face so that he blinked and opened his eyes.

Fay began to prepare breakfast, and Eddie got up. He grinned at me as he knotted his necktie, and leered: "Have a good night, Janson?"

I pleaded with him with my eyes to remove the gag. My head ached and I had a foul taste in my mouth. Eddie crowded into the kitchen with Fay, and I heard the sound of cold water splashing in the sink.

He came out wiping his face with a towel, and the smell of frying bacon began to waft in from the kitchen. Eddie combed his hair and looked spruced-up by the time that Fay brought in the coffee and the bacon and eggs. They sat down at the table together and Eddie shot an occasional mocking grin as he saw my eyes fixed hungrily on the food.

When they were through, Eddie said brusquely: "Get these things cleared away and get yourself cleaned up."

Fay washed up and spent some time powdering her face and combing her hair and straightening out the blue and white check frock, which had got crumpled the night before. Then she said quietly: "I'm ready, Eddie."

He looked at the clock and said: "You've got nice time. You'll arrive in town about ten. Just when the banks open." He put an attache case on the table and transferred to it the bunch of safe deposit keys I'd seen in his suitcase. Then he took two pieces of paper from his pocket and unfolded them. "This is a list of the seven banks," he said. "And this is a letter signed by me, authorising you to collect the vault contents on my behalf."

She glanced at the letter, and her brow clouded. "This is signed 'Robinson'," she pointed out.

"That's right," said Eddie. "That's the name I used when I deposited it."

She locked the attache case and folded the letters away in the pocket of her frock. "Leave it to me, Eddie," she said. "I'll get it."

"Don't waste any time," he snarled. "Drive straight from one bank to the other and don't waste time talking. Don't waste time counting the dough either. Just shove it in the attache case and get back as soon as you can."

"Okay, Eddie. I'll be as quick as I can." She turned her face upwards to him so he could kiss her. Her cheek was now badly discoloured, and her eye wore a halo of yellow.

"Maybe I shouldn't have hit you that hard," he said.

"It didn't matter, Eddie," she said.

"But those bank managers might think it strange," he said. "Better tell them you had an accident."

"I'll tell them," she said quietly, and she still stood there with her face upraised, waiting to be kissed. Eddie chuckled, reached out for her and kissed her on the lips. After a moment, she tore herself free from him with a short cry of pain. He had bitten her lip, and blood trickled down over her chin. He chuckled as she dabbed with her handkerchief at her torn lip and tried to hold back the tears of pain.

"Get along," Eddie said roughly. "I ain't got all day to hang about."

When she'd gone, Eddie came over to me, leered down and said: "You shouldn't have stuck your nose into this, Janson." Then he grabbed my hair, pulled my head off the pillow and, with his other hand, began to slap my face hard from side to side. He went on slapping like that, as hard as he knew how, until he got tired. Then he allowed my head to drop back on the pillow. He walked across the room, settled himself comfortably on the other bunk and began to read the magazine that Fay had discarded the night before.

I was boiling inside. Those first savage slaps had caused tears to spurt from my eyes. He had kept on after that until my cheeks felt white-hot, like the skin was burning. But what got me madder than anything was the feeling of frustration and humiliation at having to accept that face-slapping from him.

The clock slowly ticked past the seconds and the minutes. Time seemed to hang. Eddie stopped reading the magazine and started in on the bottle of whisky. He didn't pay any more attention to me, and for that I was thankful.

It musta been an hour and a half later when Fay returned. She came in looking pale and tired. She put the attache case on the table and said: "I did what you wanted, Eddie."

His eyes gleamed excitedly, and he opened the attache case and feasted his eyes on the stacks of dollar bills with which it was crammed. I could almost see him licking his lips. Then he shut the case again, locked it carefully, and put it with the suitcase.

"Want something to eat, Eddie?" Fay asked.

He was preparing to fasten a safety strap around his suitcase. He hesitated, holding the strap in his hands, and he looked at Fay thoughtfully. "No," he said, "I don't want anything to eat. It's you I want, Fay."

"Eddie," she said. "I've been longing to hear you say that."

"You know I love you, honey," he said.

She crossed to him quickly and put her arms around his neck. He put his arms around her waist, and kissed her passionately. Then his fingers began to gather up her dress, pulling the hem of it up around her waist.

She said breathlessly: "Not now, Eddie. Not while this fella's around."

"To hell with him," said Eddie thickly. "We don't have to bother about him, baby."

He pulled her frock higher, and she took her arms from around his neck and placed them across her breasts so that he could pull the frock over her head. She was still wearing her white briefs, and lower down I could see where his cruel fingers had bruised her skin.

"Wait a minute," protested Fay. "You've got to unbutton the front."

"That's all right," grunted Eddie. "I'm not bothering about that." He'd pulled her frock up tightly under her armpits, and as he drew the skirt over her head, I saw the spiteful gleam in

94

his eyes. Had it been possible, I would have shouted a warning to Fay. Eddie drew the dress over her head and arms and pulled the ends together so that it looked like she had her head in a bag. I could hear her muffled voice protesting. Eddie worked fast then. With a savage kick, he jerked her slim legs from under her, and without the help of her arms to break her fall, the white briefs thudded hard on the floor. Eddie bent quickly, seized her ankles and stood up again, pulling her legs well off the ground so that only her shoulders were touching the floor. He tucked her legs underneath his arms and used the strap to pinion her ankles together. Whilst he was doing this, Fay was struggling desperately to get the frock over her head. She managed to tear it free from her shoulders at the same time as Eddy completed the pinioning to his satisfaction.

"Eddie," she screamed. "What are you doing?"

Still keeping her legs held high off the ground and tucked under his arm, Eddie casually fumbled in the kitchen drawer and produced two lengths of cord. He nodded to himself, as though satisfied that they would serve his purpose, and then twisted hard on Fay's legs so that she was compelled to roll over onto her belly. She lay with her face cushioned against the hard floorboards and her hands spread out, trying to ease her tender body away from the rough floor. Eddie dropped her feet suddenly and sat down astride her, his heavy body grinding her bare skin hard against the wooden boards.

It was interesting the way Eddie had done this. Every move had been well thought-out and calculated to give him the least amount of trouble. Fay was a game girl, and in a tussle would have put up plenty of resistance. The way he had done it, Eddie wasn't even ruffled.

He sat there quite calmly, taking his time as he carefully knotted one of the cords to each of her wrists. All the time, she was pleading desperately with him to let her get up. "Okay, Fay," he said at last, "you can get up."

He stood up, taking his weight off her but being careful to hold in each hand the lengths of cord leading to her wrists. For a moment she lay there too exhausted to move. Then, wearily, she pushed herself up into a sitting position. That was what Eddie was waiting for. He bent down quickly, crossed the cords around her body and tugged hard. Her hands had to go with the cords. The way he'd done it meant that her arms were drawn across the front of her body.

"Eddie," she screamed.

All that appeal got from Eddie was a chuckle. He rammed his knee in the centre of her back and strained with all the strength he could summon. When he'd tied the cord and Fay desperately struggled to uncross her arms, the cord cut deeply into her back. Eddie dusted off his hands with affection, opened the door and carried his suitcases outside.

When he came back, Fay had managed to climb onto her knees and was trying to get to her feet. Eddie grinned and pushed her gently with his foot, and she toppled over again. I was mad about that. I'd known all the time that I myself could have got to my feet if I'd wanted. But it wouldn't have got me anywhere. Not at the time. But it might have helped later. All Fay had done was to remind Eddie that, tied the way we were, we could still get around.

Eddie crossed to the window, ripped down the curtains and began to stuff them into the cracks between the windows and the window ledge. He did the same with the other window, and then looked at the door reflectively. "I can plug that from outside," he said, and gave Fay another casual shove with his foot. She toppled over for the second time.

"Eddie," she shouted frantically. "What are you doing? What are you up to?"

He looked at me thoughtfully. "You've served your purpose, Fay," he said, absently. He was thinking of other things. "I think we'll have you on the floor, Mr Janson," he sneered.

I tried to kick out at him as he came across me. He chuckled, circled around my kicking legs and, with a swift jerk, tumbled me onto the floor. I fell heavily, and on my face. My chin and nose hit the floor at the same time. I thought I really was gonna suffocate then, because my nose was filled with blood and blocked the air passages.

But, for reasons that were apparent later, Eddie rolled me over and, with agonising slowness, peeled the plaster away from my lips. It felt like every hair on my chin had been plucked out with it. I snorted, spat out blood, which had trickled into my throat, and gulped in air thankfully.

"Shouting won't do any good, Janson," he said. "And don't be so stupid, honey," he added, annoyed.

Fay had got to her knees once again, and Eddie rested his foot against her shoulder and thrust hard. With her arms tied across her body the way they were, she couldn't save herself. Her cheek and her shoulder hit the floor at the same time, and this time she was smart enough not to try it again.

"Very primitive, these places," said Eddie conversationally. "Electric light, telephone and running water. But no proper sewerage, and only Calor gas for cooking." He shrugged eloquently. "But, even so, every disadvantage can be turned to an advantage."

"What are you getting at?" I asked grimly. Deep down inside my mind, I had an uneasy suspicion of what he meant. But I didn't want to think he meant it.

But he did!

"Gas is heavier than air," he said. "So to make it quicker for you both, it'll be better if you remain on the floor."

"You swine," I snarled at him. "You don't have to go that far. Even if you wanna keep me quiet, you don't have to kill the dame as well."

"But I do," he assured me seriously. "I do."

Then I knew that my hunch was right, and it was then that I began to call myself every kind of dope for walking into this right up to my neck without trying to provide cover for myself. But I guess every damn fool reporter who wants an exclusive story just can't help doing that kinda fool trick.

Fay was half hysterical now. She kept moaning Eddie's name over and over and over again. Quite unflurried, Eddie took a handful of her long hair and dragged her across the floor to lie alongside me. "How convenient," he chuckled as he fingered Fay's long, silky hair.

Fay was lying alongside me with her head at my feet. Eddie threaded thick strands of Fay's long hair through the cords that held my ankles together, and knotted it securely. He tested the knots to make sure they wouldn't come loose.

"Everything seems most convenient," he commented again, and he took the ends of my tie, passed them around Fay's ankles, and knotted them securely together.

"Listen, Eddie," I pleaded desperately. "Leave the dame outta this, will you? Take her with you. It won't do no harm."

"Eddie, Eddie, don't leave me," she moaned.

"I'm afraid," said Eddie casually, "that I've had enough of this dame. She doesn't interest me no more." He looked around carefully, as though checking everything. "I don't think there's anything else. Is there?" he asked me, looking at me with a mocking smile.

"I wish there was," I said bitterly.

"Well, that's that then," he said with cheerful satisfaction.

He stepped into the kitchen, and I watched him turn on all the taps of the small caravan gas-stove. There were three large cylinders of gas, all connected to the one stove. There was enough compressed gas there to fill the cabin to a height of ten feet. But neither Fay nor I would know anything about how high it got.

"I'll be getting along now," said Eddie.

"You can't leave me, Eddie," shrieked Fay desperately, and she began struggling. I didn't know if she pulled her hair out by the roots, but I did know that I was nearly strangled as her kicking legs caused my tie to bite deeper into my neck.

"You won't miss me, Fay," said Eddie. He picked up the attache case holding the money. "I do hope it won't take too long," he added considerately.

Fay began screaming desperately, struggling madly to get to her feet, enduring untold agonies herself and choking the life out of me.

Eddie chuckled as he opened the door.

CHAPTER NINE

Trice opened the door, but he didn't go out. Instead, for a startled moment, he stood stock still. Then he backed a coupla paces and moved his hands towards his pockets.

"Why, Lynn," he said nervously. "This is a surprise!"

Yeah. It was Lynn. She musta been about to knock. As Eddie opened the door, he almost walked into her. She was wearing a white mackintosh, and her right hand was in her pocket. Her face was white and set like I'd never seen before. Somehow, I could sense her deadliness of purpose.

Eddie said: "I wasn't expecting you, Lynn," and, at the same time, his hand lifted the flap of his pocket and began to slide inside.

"Watch it, Lynn," I yelled. "He's gotta gun."

My shout of warning musta startled Eddie. He dived for his gun, trying to rip it from his pocket. He wasted valuable seconds that way. Maybe he misjudged the calibre of the woman he was dealing with.

Lynn didn't wait for him to get his gun out. She fired herself, with a cold, ruthless kinda deadliness. It couldn't have been a very big gat, as it didn't make much noise. Eddie gave a kinda grunt, and the gun he was trying to level fell from his fingers. It clattered loudly on the floorboards, and for a second or two the whole world seemed poised in space.

I looked at the gun that had fallen on the floor close by me. Then I looked up at Lynn's white face, and my eyes slid down to the tiny brown hole just above her pocket, from which spiralled a thin wisp of smoke.

Eddie grunted again, stepped back a coupla paces, felt behind him for a chair and sat down heavily. His face had become quite white, and there was a dull, pained, startled look in his eyes. He was clasping both hands to his belly as though he was afraid his innards were gonna drop on the floor.

"Get that other gun, Lynn," I yelled warningly.

But I didn't need to worry that she wouldn't know how to handle this. She bent down for Eddie's gun. But not once did she take her eyes off his face. But the way he was, it didn't look like he was gonna raise any argument, anyway.

"Cut me loose, Lynn," I said urgently. "Let me take over. You can't handle this alone."

"Where's the knife?"

"In the table drawer," I said. "Better watch him, just in case."

She circled around the table, keeping the gun pointed at Eddie, and got a knife from the drawer. She was still watching him as she sawed through the cords around my hands and ankles. As soon as I got to my feet and fought off sufficiently the pain of returning circulation, I took the gun from her hand. "Turn the gas-jets off in the kitchen," I ordered. "Then you'd better get Fay loose."

Lynn was acting like an automaton now. She was a different dame from the one I knew. Now she was a cold, hard dame. And I knew she was using all her strength to keep a grip on herself so she wouldn't break down. She did all that I told her to, calmly and without undue haste.

"How d'you feel, Eddie?" I asked.

He looked up at me, and there was still that startled, surprised look in his eyes. "She shot me," he said. He sounded like he couldn't believe it had happened.

"Is that where it got you?" I said, nodding towards his belly.

He nodded. He seemed afraid to move his hands.

I moved close to him, and he looked at me appealingly. Suddenly I knew I didn't have to worry about Eddie trying anything funny. I put the gun on the mantelpiece, unbuttoned his coat and shirt and pulled up his vest. There was a small hole just above the trouser line, from which thick, dark blood was oozing. It didn't look very pleasant, and I knew that there was nothing I could do about it.

I went across to the telephone and asked the operator for my hotel. Cleve Sanders, the Marshal, was waiting in my room for me to telephone. He had Jake Peters with him. I gave him the address, told him to get over as soon as he knew how, and to bring an ambulance.

"What goes on?" he asked.

"Don't waste time," I yelled at him. "Every minute counts." I gave a sidelong glance at Eddie. His face looked grey and there was pain sweat on his forehead. He didn't look like a man who'd last long to me. "Fast as hell," I repeated, and hung up.

As soon as Lynn released her, Fay would have thrown herself onto Eddie, clinging to him, trying to hug him. I jerked her back. "Take it easy," I yelled. "You've gotta treat him gentle. He's hurt, can't you see?"

She kinda flinched back, and then fell down on her knees so she could bury her face on his lap. "Eddie," she moaned. "Eddie, darling. I love you. Don't leave me. Don't ever leave me." She burst into a fit of sobbing, and after a time, she looked at me pleadingly. "Are you getting a doctor?" she asked.

I patted her on the shoulder. "He's on his way," I said.

Eddie's arms were hanging limply at his sides now. He looked down at Fay, and his eyes flicked up towards me. He moistened his lips with his tongue and said hoarsely: "Give me a shot, will you?"

"Pour him a drink, will ya, Lynn?" I said.

I saw the way her hands shook as she poured. "Better have one yourself," I said. "Make it a good one."

It was terrible waiting there for the others to arrive. Fay kept clinging on to his legs and sobbing that she loved him, and Lynn got the shakes so badly that she had to sit down on the bunk and try to control herself.

I don't think I've every been so thankful as I was when I heard car brakes squeal outside and when Sanders and Jake Peters came bursting in.

Sanders gave one look at Eddie and said in amazement: "Tundall. Damn it. It's Tundall!"

Jake Peters gave a low cackle. "What did I tell you, Cleve?" he gloated. "What did I tell you? I knew I'd seen him after everybody said he'd been murdered."

"Where's the doctor?" I asked crisply.

"Right here," said Cleve, as the doctor shouldered him to one side.

I didn't say anything. I just pointed at Eddie. Lynn took Fay by the shoulder and led her across the room while the doctor conducted his examination.

When he was through, he looked over his glasses meaningfully at the Marshal and walked outside. The Marshal followed him and returned a few moments later. He caught my eye and whispered: "Doc says there's nothing he can do. Probably won't last until we get to hospital."

"Maybe I can straighten out one or two things right now," I said. I added significantly: "If we don't do it now, we might never do it."

Cleve looked at me thoughtfully; his eyes flicked across to Eddie. Then he looked back at me again. "Make it snappy, son," he said.

I went across and stood by Eddie. "How ya feeling, fella?" I asked.

He didn't look up. He just said slowly: "Like hell."

"I hate to press it at a time like this, Eddie," I said. "But we want to straighten out a few things."

"It's finished," he said hoarsely. "Everything's finished."

101

I looked at the Marshal. "It's like this, Sanders," I said. "Five years ago, Eddie got a three years' stretch. At the time, he was running a one-man stock-broking office, which paid off well. But when he went behind bars, his connection and his business finished. He got a year's remission for good conduct, and three years ago, when he was released, he came to Benton, where, with the help of influential friends, he got a job at City Hall."

"I knew there was something queer about him not having a previous record," said the Marshal.

"This is all conjecture," I said. "But Eddie can speak up if I'm not stating the facts." I looked at Eddie questioningly.

"Carry on," he said wearily. "You seem to know it all."

"Eddie wasn't content to remain a mere accountant at the City Hall. As jobs go, he had a good job. But Eddie was accustomed to money and he wanted money. Plenty of it! It was that driving desire that got him scheming and planning right up until the day he made a phoney call and got Johnny Peters driving out to a breakdown that never existed.

"While Johnny Peters was away, and having previously taken care to inform everybody where he was going, Eddie drove over to Peters' garage, found a loose floorboard, and beneath it hid the blood-stained axe and the money he had already drawn out from the bank. The money was to suggest a motive for crime."

"How about the blood-stains on the axe?" asked Sanders.

"Eddy's got a cut on his wrist. It's an unusual place to cut yourself. It's an unusual cut, too. It's the kinda cut that looks like a slit by a razor-blade. A cut like that would bleed plenty, and it's easy to pluck a few hairs from your head.

Jake said excitedly: "That's it, young fella. He framed my Johnny. That's what he did."

"Pretty clever acting," I agreed. "Well thought out. Platinum, lead and gold don't dissolve in acid. Eddie knew that and deliberately dropped his gold ring and watch medallion into the vat of acid. Just as make-weight, to give the analyst something satisfactory, he probably dropped in some old clothing together with some raw meat. It might be worth your while, Marshal, to check at butchers' shops to see if Eddie bought a large chunk of meat that particular day."

The Marshal scratched his head. "I don't think I'm following this, Janson. Why did he do all this?"

"I'm making another guess now," I said. "Eddie was accountant at County Hall. He'd been there three years. I bet during that time he salted away quite a lotta dough. He'd be able to cook the books to cover it up. That money he deposited in different safe vaults in different banks in Morton." I looked down at Eddie. "Am I right there?" I asked.

He made an effort and looked up at me. "Figured it out, ain't ya?" he growled.

"Now, Eddie had been to stir once," I went on, "and he didn't like it. Nobody does. And Eddie knew that sooner or later it would be discovered that money had been embezzled. There'd be a hue and cry after him then."

"And so he decided to get himself murdered then," said Sanders, suddenly understanding.

I nodded. "Once he was dead, nobody'd ever try to find him. He could live out his life in some other State in comfort and freedom from the thought of imprisonment."

Sanders looked levelly at Eddie. "It's lucky for you that young Peters ain't here," he said. "He wouldn't like the idea of being sent to the chair as a cover-up for you."

Eddie rested his eyes on the Marshal, licked his lips and then, amazingly, managed to smile. "What do I care for Peters, or any of you?" he asked.

I said: "His scheming didn't finish there. Although he'd been at great pains to conceal his real identity in Benton, not even allowing a single photograph of himself to exist, there was always the possibility that police enquiries might get as far afield as Morton. If, somewhere, there'd been a photograph that had been overlooked and that was circulated, it might have put the finger on him when he went to collect the money from the safe deposits. So far, the Morton banks knew him by name only. He'd sent all his deposits to them by registered post.

"The only safe way was to get somebody else to call at the banks for him. But there, Eddie was stumped. There was nobody he knew whom he could trust. They would either collect the money and go take a powder with it or, at best, if they collected the money and returned it to Eddie, they would want a half-share and maybe blackmail him later.

"Then Eddie recalled the one person whom he could trust. The one person who would follow out his instructions, return faithfully with the money and expect to receive none of it." I looked at Fay. "There she is over there," I said. "She used to be his wife."

"Did she get the money?" asked Sanders.

I picked up the attache case, which Eddie had dropped on the floor when he'd been shot, and forced it open. There were gasps of amazement as they saw that it was crammed full with dollar bills.

"What a haul!" said Sanders.

"Yeah, that's what Eddie thought when he saw it. And by that time, I'd got myself tangled with him, and he knew that he'd have to keep me quiet. Eddie figured he might as well be hanged for a sheep as for a lamb. There's no knowing now; he might have taken a trip with the dame, or he might have bumped her off anyway. But as I had to be liquidated anyway, he decided to make a duet of it."

I exhibited my wrists, torn by the cords, pointed at the windows that had been plugged up, and said: "The Calor gas is over there – Lynn got here in time. He'd have killed her, too. He almost did. But Lynn knew the type of man he was. She was smart enough to come ready for him, and she got in first."

The doctor came back then. "The ambulance has arrived," he said.

"Better take him," said Sanders.

The doctor walked across to Eddie, who was staring with glazed eyes at the floor. The colour seemed to have come back to his cheeks. "We're gonna take you to hospital, fella," he said. "Think you can make it?"

Eddie went on staring at the floor.

"Think you can make it?" repeated the doctor a little more loudly.

Eddie still stared at the floor.

The doctor leaned forward. He reached out and felt for Eddie's wrist. A few moments later he straightened up and said: "Funny thing, ain't it. Some look better – dead!"

From Fay's corner came a wild shriek of horror, followed by a spasm of bitter weeping. The doctor shrugged his shoulders, pushed past us and held up a restraining hand to the white-coated orderlies who were bringing in a stretcher. "Job for the morgue," he said. "Let them send their own wagon."

Cleve looked around. "Looks like we'll have to wait for the casket."

"Sorry it had to be this way," I said. "If Eddie could have made a confession, it would have been easier."

Fay was weeping more quietly now. Lynn was comforting her.

"The way you tell it sounds okay to me," said Sanders. "It all matches in."

Jake Peters dug me hard with a long forefinger. "There's a lot I don't understand, young man," he said. "What put you on to this guy, anyway?"

"Yeah," said Sanders. "Just what made you figure it out this way?"

"Little bits and pieces," I said. "Obviously, the first thing that gave me the hunch was when Jake Peters said he had seen Tundall in Morton three days after he was supposed to have been murdered. Everybody thought Jake Peters was a crackpot and wouldn't listen to him."

Jake Peters gave a cackle of laughter. He broke off suddenly and stared apologetically at Eddie.

"Then the evidence against Johnny Peters seemed just too good to be true. Everything was laid on. Johnny had no alibi; the dough was found in his shack, dough that had been drawn from the bank the same day and all the numbers noted; and there was the blood-stained axe. It was too good a case against Johnny. Well, that wasn't much to work on. And then I went chasing after Fay, which I thought was completely unconnected with Johnny Peters. But the moment I met Fay's husband, it struck me right away that he fitted in with Jake's description of Tundall.

"I noticed, too, that he had a bandaged wrist. I didn't think overmuch of it at the time. And I'd only noticed that Eddie bore a resemblance to Tundall. Right then, I never connected him as being the same person. But I had to tangle with Eddie on account of Fay. That gave me the opportunity to learn about the deposit accounts and to hear Eddie give the Marshal of Benton his full name, Cleve Sanders, proving that he knew at least one man in Benton. That's when I made my long shot."

"It's the longest shot that I've ever heard of," said Sanders. He looked at Lynn, who was still comforting Fay, and then grimaced at me and jerked his head towards the door. I nodded and followed him outside. He said: "Lucky break for you that the dame turned up when she did."

"Lucky for me – and her sister."

He looked down at his feet and cleared his throat nervously. "I'll have to charge her, you know," he said. "It'll be only a formality. The case will be dismissed as self-defence. Perhaps you'd better break it to her gently."

"I think she knows the implications of what she's done," I said quietly. "She knew what she had to do, and she did it. But she hated every moment of it."

Sanders rubbed his chin. "I've got my duty to do," he said awkwardly. "I ought to tell her right away where she stands. How do you think she'll take it?"

"She'll take it all right," I said. I patted him on the arm. "I'll get her," I said.

I poked my head inside the cabin and yelled: "Lynn, can you step outside for a minute?"

She came out a few seconds later. Her face was still white and set, and as soon as she saw the Marshal's face, she knew what he wanted.

"Am I under arrest?" she asked simply.

"No, miss," he drawled. "That ain't gonna be necessary. And I don't want you to worry yourself about it. There's going to be nothing to it, but–"

The sound of the shot was as loud as it was sudden. For seconds we froze there, and then Sanders ran back into the cabin. Lynn rushed after him. I grabbed her around the waist and held her back. She struggled desperately, but I held on to her tightly. I guessed what that shot meant, and Lynn had seen too much unpleasantness for one day already.

"Let me go," she panted. "I've gotta go to her."

I held on to her tightly but didn't say anything. There was nothing to say.

There was still nothing to say when Sanders reappeared in the doorway. He looked at me, he looked at Lynn and then he looked at Jake Peters. "Listen, folks," he said quietly, "there's no need for us to be hanging around here. Let's get back to town."

Lynn choked back a sob of horror. "She couldn't have," she cried protestingly. "She couldn't have done that!"

The Marshal looked down at the toes of his boots. "You don't want to go in there, miss," he said. "It's not very pretty."

Lynn turned around and buried her face on my shoulder. I tried to comfort her as her body shook with great sobs that came bubbling up into her throat from way down inside her.

The Marshal caught my eye. "I'll get the car," he said quietly. "There's no point in staying. Better to get away from here."

After we had been driving for a few minutes, Lynn took my hand. I had my other arm around her, trying to comfort her.

"Howya feeling now, honey?" I asked.

"It was such a shock."

"Of course," I said soothingly.

There was silence for a few seconds, and then she turned her eyes upwards to mine. Her face was still white, and her cheeks were wet. But there was no despairing look in her eyes. Instead, her eyes seemed to sparkle, alive with hope and understanding.

"Maybe some people don't know so much," she said.

"Meaning what?"

"That man," she said. "He deserved to die. He was a beast."

"Forget about it, honey," I suggested.

"But maybe Fay was happier than we'll ever know," she said intensely. Her eyes searched mine. "Maybe she was richer than we'll ever be."

I frowned at her, not understanding.

"It must be wonderful to love so deeply," she said. "Even to love a beast like Trice. It must be wonderful to love anyone so much that you cannot bear to live without them."

"I wonder if that can be so," I mused. "I wonder."

106

Also available from Telos Publishing

DOCTOR WHO NOVELLAS

DOCTOR WHO: TIME AND RELATIVE by KIM NEWMAN

The harsh British winter of 1962/3 brings a big freeze and with it comes a new, far greater menace: terrifying icy creatures are stalking the streets, bringing death and destruction.

An adventure featuring the first Doctor and Susan.
Featuring a foreword by Justin Richards.
Deluxe edition frontispiece by Bryan Talbot.
SOLD OUT Standard h/b ISBN: 1-903889-02-2
£25 (+ £1.50 UK p&p) Deluxe h/b ISBN: 1-903889-03-0

DOCTOR WHO: CITADEL OF DREAMS by DAVE STONE

In the city-state of Hokesh, time plays tricks; the present is unreliable, the future impossible to intimate.

An adventure featuring the seventh Doctor and Ace.
Featuring a foreword by Andrew Cartmel.
Deluxe edition frontispiece by Lee Sullivan.
£10 (+ £1.50 UK p&p) Standard h/b ISBN: 1-903889-04-9
£25 (+ £1.50 UK p&p) Deluxe h/b ISBN: 1-903889-05-7

DOCTOR WHO: NIGHTDREAMERS by TOM ARDEN

Perihelion Night on the wooded moon Verd. A time of strange sightings, ghosts, and celebration. But what of the mysterious and terrifying Nightdreamers? And of the Nightdreamer King?

An adventure featuring the third Doctor and Jo.
Featuring a foreword by Katy Manning.
Deluxe edition frontispiece by Martin McKenna.
£10 (+ £1.50 UK p&p) Standard h/b ISBN: 1-903889-06-5
£25 (+ £1.50 UK p&p) Deluxe h/b ISBN: 1-903889-07-3

DOCTOR WHO: GHOST SHIP by KEITH TOPPING

The TARDIS lands in the most haunted place on Earth, the luxury ocean liner the Queen Mary on its way from Southampton to New York in the year 1963. But why do ghosts from the past, the present and, perhaps even the future, seek out the Doctor?

An adventure featuring the fourth Doctor.
Featuring a foreword by Hugh Lamb.
Deluxe edition frontispiece by Dariusz Jasiczak.
£5.99 (+ £1.50 UK p&p) p/b ISBN: 1-903889-32-4
SOLD OUT Standard h/b ISBN: 1-903889-08-1
£25 (+ £1.50 UK p&p) Deluxe h/b ISBN: 1-903889-09-X

DOCTOR WHO: FOREIGN DEVILS by ANDREW CARTMEL

The Doctor, Jamie and Zoe find themselves joining forces with a psychic investigator named Carnacki to solve a series of strange murders in an English country house.

An adventure featuring the second Doctor, Jamie and Zoe.

Featuring a foreword by Mike Ashley.

Deluxe edition frontispiece by Mike Collins.

£5.99 (+ £1.50 UK p&p) p/b ISBN: 1-903889-33-2

SOLD OUT Standard h/b ISBN: 1-903889-10-3

£25 (+ £1.50 UK p&p) Deluxe h/b ISBN: 1-903889-11-1

DOCTOR WHO: RIP TIDE by LOUISE COOPER

Strange things are afoot in a sleepy Cornish village. Strangers are hanging about the harbour and a mysterious object is retrieved from the sea bed. Then the locals start getting sick. The Doctor is perhaps the only person who can help, but can he discover the truth in time?

An adventure featuring the eighth Doctor.

Featuring a foreword by Stephen Gallagher.

Deluxe edition frontispiece by Fred Gambino.

£10 (+ £1.50 UK p&p) Standard h/b ISBN: 1-903889-12-X

£25 (+ £1.50 UK p&p) Deluxe h/b ISBN: 1-903889-13-8

DOCTOR WHO: WONDERLAND by MARK CHADBOURN

San Francisco 1967. A place of love and peace as the hippy movement is in full swing. Summer, however, has lost her boyfriend, and fears him dead, destroyed by a new type of drug nicknamed Blue Moonbeams. Her only friends are three English tourists: Ben and Polly, and the mysterious Doctor. But will any of them help Summer, and what is the strange threat posed by the Blue Moonbeams?

An adventure featuring the second Doctor, Ben and Polly.

Featuring a foreword by Graham Joyce.

Deluxe edition frontispiece by Dominic Harman.

£10 (+ £1.50 UK p&p) Standard h/b ISBN: 1-903889-14-6

£25 (+ £1.50 UK p&p) Deluxe h/b ISBN: 1-903889-15-4

DOCTOR WHO: SHELL SHOCK by SIMON A. FORWARD

The Doctor is stranded on an alien beach with only intelligent crabs and a madman for company. How can he possibly rescue Peri, who was lost at sea the same time as he and the TARDIS?

An adventure featuring the sixth Doctor and Peri.

Featuring a foreword by Guy N. Smith.

Deluxe edition frontispiece by Bob Covington.

£10 (+ £1.50 UK p&p) Standard h/b ISBN: 1-903889-16-2

£25 (+ £1.50 UK p&p) Deluxe h/b ISBN: 1-903889-17-0

DOCTOR WHO: THE CABINET OF LIGHT
by DANIEL O'MAHONY

Where is the Doctor? Everyone is hunting him. Honoré Lechasseur, a time sensitive 'fixer', is hired by mystery woman Emily Blandish to find him. But what is his connection with London in 1949? Lechasseur is about to discover that following in the Doctor's footsteps can be a difficult task.

An adventure featuring the Doctor.

Featuring a foreword by Chaz Brenchley.

Deluxe edition frontispiece by John Higgins.

£10 (+ £1.50 UK p&p) Standard h/b ISBN: 1-903889-18-9

£25 (+ £1.50 UK p&p) Deluxe h/b ISBN: 1-903889-19-7

DOCTOR WHO: FALLEN GODS
by KATE ORMAN and JONATHAN BLUM

In ancient Akrotiri, a young girl is learning the mysteries of magic from a tutor, who, quite literally, fell from the skies. With his encouragement she can surf the timestreams and see something of the future. But then the demons come.

An adventure featuring the eighth Doctor

Featuring a foreword by Storm Constantine.

Deluxe edition frontispiece by Daryl Joyce.

£10 (+ £1.50 UK p&p) Standard h/b ISBN: 1-903889-20-1

£25 (+ £1.50 UK p&p) Deluxe h/b ISBN: 1-903889-21-9

DOCTOR WHO: FRAYED by TARA SAMMS

On a blasted world, the Doctor and Susan find themselves in the middle of a war they cannot understand. With Susan missing and the Doctor captured, who will save the people from the enemies both from outside and within?

An adventure featuring the first Doctor and Susan.

Featuring a foreword by Stephen Laws.

Deluxe edition frontispiece by Chris Moore.

£10 (+ £1.50 UK p&p) Standard h/b ISBN: 1-903889-22-7

£25 (+ £1.50 UK p&p) Deluxe h/b ISBN: 1-903889-23-5

DOCTOR WHO: EYE OF THE TYGER by PAUL MCAULEY

On a spaceship trapped in the orbit of a black hole, the Doctor finds himself fighting to save a civilisation from extinction.

An adventure featuring the eighth Doctor.

Featuring a foreword by Neil Gaiman.

Deluxe edition frontispiece by Jim Burns.

£10 (+ £1.50 UK p&p) Standard h/b ISBN: 1-903889-24-3

£25 (+ £1.50 UK p&p) Deluxe h/b ISBN: 1-903889-25-1

Published November 2003

DOCTOR WHO: COMPANION PIECE
by MIKE TUCKER and ROBERT PERRY

The Doctor and his companion Cat face insurmountable odds when the Doctor is accused of the crime of time travelling and taken to Rome to face the Papal Inquisition.

An adventure featuring the seventh Doctor and Cat.

Featuring a foreword by TBA.

Deluxe edition frontispiece by Allan Bednar.

£10 (+ £1.50 UK p&p) Standard h/b ISBN: 1-903889-26-X

£25 (+ £1.50 UK p&p) Deluxe h/b ISBN: 1-903889-27-8

Published December 2003

TIME HUNTER

A new range of high-quality original paperback novellas featuring the adventures in time of Honoré Lechasseur. Part mystery, part detective story, part dark fantasy, part science fiction … these books are guaranteed to enthrall fans of good fiction everywhere, and are in the spirit of our acclaimed range of *Doctor Who* Novellas.

THE WINNING SIDE by LANCE PARKIN

Emily is dead! Killed by an unknown assailant. Honoré and Emily find themselves caught up in a plot reaching from the future to their past, and with their very existence, not to mention the future of the entire world, at stake, can they unravel the mystery before it is too late?

An adventure in time and space.

£8 (+ £1.50 UK p&p) Standard p/b ISBN: 1-903889-35-9

£25 (+ £1.50 UK p&p) Deluxe h/b ISBN: 1-903889-36-7

HORROR/FANTASY

URBAN GOTHIC: LACUNA & OTHER TRIPS
ed. DAVID J. HOWE

Stories by Graham Masterton, Christopher Fowler, Simon Clark, Debbie Bennett, Paul Finch, Steve Lockley & Paul Lewis.

Based on the Channel 5 horror series.

SOLD OUT

THE MANITOU by GRAHAM MASTERTON

A 25th Anniversary author's preferred edition of this classic horror novel. An ancient Red Indian medicine man is reincarnated in modern day New York intent on reclaiming his land from the white men.

£9.99 (+ £2.50 p&p) Standard p/b ISBN: 1-903889-70-7
£30.00 (+ £2.50 p&p) Deluxe h/b ISBN: 1-903889-71-5

CAPE WRATH by PAUL FINCH

Death and horror on a deserted Scottish island as an ancient Viking warrior chief returns to life.

£8.00 (+ £1.50 p&p) Standard p/b ISBN: 1-903889-60-X

KING OF ALL THE DEAD by STEVE LOCKLEY & PAUL LEWIS

The king of all the dead will have what is his.

£8.00 (+ £1.50 p&p) Standard p/b ISBN: 1-903889-61-8

GUARDIAN ANGEL by STEPHANIE BEDWELL-GRIME

Devilish fun as Guardian Angel Porsche Winter loses a soul to the devil ...

£9.99 (+ £2.50 p&p) Standard p/b ISBN: 1-903889-62-6

TV/FILM GUIDES

BEYOND THE GATE: THE UNAUTHORISED AND UNOFFICIAL GUIDE TO STARGATE SG-1 by KEITH TOPPING

Complete episode guide to the middle of Season 6 of the popular TV show.

£9.99 (+ £2.50 p&p) Standard p/b ISBN: 1-903889-50-2

A DAY IN THE LIFE: THE UNAUTHORISED AND UNOFFICIAL GUIDE TO 24 by KEITH TOPPING

Complete episode guide to the first season of the popular TV show.

£9.99 (+ £2.50 p&p) Standard p/b ISBN: 1-903889-53-7

THE TELEVISION COMPANION: THE UNAUTHORISED AND UNOFFICIAL GUIDE TO DOCTOR WHO by DAVID J HOWE & STEPHEN JAMES WALKER

Complete episode guide to the popular TV show.

£14.99 (+ £4.00 p&p) Standard p/b ISBN: 1-903889-51-0
£30.00 (+ £4.00 p&p) Deluxe h/b ISBN: 1-903889-52-9

LIBERATION: THE UNAUTHORISED AND UNOFFICIAL GUIDE TO BLAKE'S 7 by ALAN STEVENS & FIONA MOORE

Complete episode guide to the popular TV show.

£9.99 (+ £2.50 p&p) Standard p/b ISBN: 1-903889-54-5
£30.00 (+ £2.50 p&p) Deluxe h/b ISBN: 1-903889-55-3

HANK JANSON

Classic pulp crime thrillers from the 1950s.

TORMENT by HANK JANSON
£9.99 (+ £2.50 p&p) Standard p/b ISBN: 1-903889-80-4

WOMEN HATE TILL DEATH by HANK JANSON
£9.99 (+ £2.50 p&p) Standard p/b ISBN: 1-903889-81-2

SKIRTS BRING ME SORROW by HANK JANSON
£9.99 (+ £2.50 p&p) Standard p/b ISBN: 1-903889-83-9

The prices shown are correct at time of going to press. However, the publishers reserve the right to increase prices from those previously advertised without prior notice.

TELOS PUBLISHING
c/o Beech House,
Chapel Lane,
Moulton,
Cheshire,
CW9 8PQ,
England
Email: orders@telos.co.uk
Web: www.telos.co.uk

To order copies of any Telos books, please visit our website where there are full details of all titles and facilities for worldwide credit card online ordering, or send a cheque or postal order (UK only) for the appropriate amount (including postage and packing), together with details of the book(s) you require, plus your name and address to the above address. Overseas readers please send two international reply coupons for details of prices and postage rates.